# FURY FREED

## Of Fates and Furies
### Book 3

# MELISSA HAAG

*To Halloween candy and ice cream,*
*Thank you for being there for me during the editing process.*

While preparing to leave Uttira after graduation, Megan finds the *Book of Fury*. The answers she's needed about who she is, her purpose, and her powers have been there the whole time, along with a shocking revelation. Now, it's not just a matter of finding Megan's mother. Megan must find the two preceding generations as well because the book is clear on one thing: there can only be three furies.

CHAPTER ONE

I stared down at the thin *Book of Fury* gripped in my hands. Finally, I had the book containing all the answers I'd been seeking. However, the fact that it had been in my house all along stirred my rage. I wanted to throw it. I wanted to yell and scream. Instead, I stood shaking uncontrollably as I waited for Oanen.

Eliana said something behind me, but the sound of my heart pounding hard in my ears and my own thoughts drowned out her words. Her arms wrapped around me, and an immediate peaceful nothingness filled me.

"How are you going to survive out there without me?" Eliana asked, resting her head against my back. "Just because some dumb book says you need to kill your great-grandma, doesn't mean you have to. You have a choice. We always have a choice."

I exhaled heavily and set my hand on her forearm. She, better than anyone, knew the truth to those words.

"You're right. I do have a choice. It's just so infuriating, you know? All that time I was looking for answers, they were right in this house. Why didn't my mom just leave the dumb book on the table? No. That would have been too easy for her to do. She probably stood in the kitchen, looking around and wondering where I would be least likely to find it." Thanks to Eliana's touch, any rage I wanted to feel slipped away from me so my words were a mellow rant.

The crunch of tires over the snow announced Oanen's arrival, and Eliana released me with a final squeeze.

"It'll be okay," she said as Oanen got out of his car.

I opened the screen door and launched myself at him before he'd made it more than two steps toward the house. He caught me in his arms and held me tightly.

"You're shaking. What's wrong?"

Burying my face in the curve of his neck, I said nothing for a moment. The desperation to feel his arms around me faded as his fingers made little circles on my back.

"I hate my mom."

His fingers stilled.

"That's the first time I've heard you say that. Why now?"

I pulled back and showed him the book.

"*Book of Fury*?" His gaze met mine. "Where did you find it?"

"Here. In the library I never used. It has everything, Oanen. All the shit that I put up with these last few months...all the fear...none of it was necessary. She could have just handed me this damn book and told me to read it."

Ignoring the book, he wrapped me in his arms again and pressed his lips to my temple.

"I'm sorry for everything you've gone through. What your mom did wasn't right. But don't hate her. If you'd had all the answers, would you have needed to come here? Would you have tried leaving your house the night I met you? Because of her, I have you, Megan."

I pulled back and looked up into his beautiful blue eyes.

"You're really good at melting my heart," I said just before brushing my lips against his.

His hold on me tightened as he kissed me. When I pulled back, I was breathless and grinning like an idiot. His now golden eyes watched me closely.

"I love when they do that," I said, reaching up to gently trace the skin near his eye.

"And I love when yours glow, which they've been doing since you walked out the door. It makes me wonder if finding the book is the only thing upsetting you." His gaze briefly flicked to something behind me.

I turned to look at Eliana, who watched me with concern and a hint of black in her eyes.

"I know what she means to you," he said. "We don't have to leave today. You and Eliana can spend some more time together."

Giving Oanen another quick hug, I threaded my fingers through his and shook my head.

"I'll miss her, but I know I'll be back." I looked down at the book. "At least, I think I will be."

"It's the book that's upsetting her, Oanen," Eliana said from the back door. "The thing says she needs to kill her great-grandma. I told her it's bull pucky. No book should dictate her life."

"Bull pucky? Wow, Eliana. I didn't know you felt so

strongly about it." I grinned widely as Oanen and I started toward the house.

"Shut up," she said with an answering smile.

Eliana opened the door for us, and I shivered slightly as I stepped into the heat. Since releasing my power on the beach the night before, my internal thermometer felt out of whack. I was never too warm anymore. If anything, I felt any chill much faster now. Not that I cared since I could finally touch Oanen without burning him.

"Can I see the book?" Oanen asked, kicking off his shoes, a sure sign we were staying for a while.

"Of course." I handed it over and took off my own shoes.

"I'm going to get going," Eliana said before I could move toward the table.

"Why?"

"Being sad makes me hungry, and you two are way more than I'll be able to resist."

I didn't bother trying to tell her I wouldn't mind if she took a little of the energy Oanen and I put off. She'd already made her stance on that very clear.

"Call me. Every day," she said, pulling me into a quick hug again. "I mean it. Or I'll worry."

"Yes, Mom," I teased. "I'll be back before you know it."

"You better be. This place is going to suck without you guys around."

"Suck? Like, what kind of suck are we talking here?"

Her mouth dropped open, and she blushed profusely.

"I changed my mind. I'm glad you're leaving."

"Whatever. You love me, and you know it. Besides, I'm helping. Every time you even get a little depressed, you're going to think about sucking. That'll motivate you to keep busy and happy so your mind doesn't go where you don't want it to."

"You're so twisted," she said, shaking her head at me.

"I know."

Despite my smile, I gloomily watched as Eliana walked out and quietly closed the door. I'd miss the hell out of her while we were gone.

Turning to Oanen, I found him frowning at the book.

"Most of the stuff in the middle is boring," I said. "Go to the last page."

He did, and I watched his eyes skim the words.

"Have you called her?" he asked, looking up.

"Call her?" My stomach churned at the thought. "What would I say? 'Hi, Paxton. Remember me? The kid you ditched a few months back. What the hell is up with this note you left in the book you hid?'"

"Yeah. Say exactly that. She owes you answers, and this book and note don't help."

I thought about what he said for a moment then reached for my phone. My stomach continued to twist as I paced the kitchen and listened to the call dial through.

Mom picked up on the second ring.

"Hello?"

It was hard to hear her over the heavy sound of traffic.

"Mom? It's Megan. I can barely hear you. Where are you?"

"New York. Hold on. Let me find somewhere quieter."

I waited a few moments, and the background noise became muffled.

"That's better," she said. "So, is it finally done?"

After over three months of not seeing me, no "Are you okay?" or anything else the least bit caring.

"Is what done?" I asked.

"Your great-grandmother, Irene. I left a note with the book. Didn't you read it yet, Megan?"

Her impatient tone poked at my temper. "Since I didn't know the book existed until twenty minutes ago, no, I haven't rushed out to kill my great-grandmother yet."

"Well, now you know. Hurry up and get it done. The longer you wait, the more you'll suffer."

"What do you mean? And why do you think she needs to die? And why do I have to do it?"

Silence greeted my questions. I looked at the phone and saw the call had ended. Scowling, I dialed again. It rang five times then just disconnected without the option to go to voicemail.

I tossed the phone on the table and sat across from Oanen. He reached out for my hand.

"You heard most of that?" I asked.

"All of it."

"She's in New York. What is that...maybe 8 hours away?"

"Don't dwell on it," Oanen said. "You can't change what she did, only what we do from here. What do you think she meant by you suffering?"

"Who knows with her? She's probably just making crap up, her way of making sure I'll do what she wants."

"I don't know. I read the part about gaining your powers. The book made it sound like the only way to gain them was by taking them from the oldest living fury."

"Bullshit. Look at what happened on the beach. I was in

the air and on fire. I don't burn you anymore when we kiss. I've already freed my powers."

He considered me for a moment.

"I just don't want anything to happen to you," he said finally.

"I know. I don't want anything to happen to me, either. Since the Council wants you to go to New York anyway, we'll see if we can find mommy-dearest and get some clarification at the same time, okay?"

He nodded and stood.

"Everything packed up?" he asked.

"Yep. Eliana took all the crappy, healthy food with her so it wouldn't rot and stink up the place. Everything else is like I found it."

I grabbed my bag, which had some clothes and my wallet in it. Oanen took it from me and held the door. It felt weird to finally be leaving the place that kept me a prisoner for so long.

"I thought you'd be happier right now," Oanen said.

"I was just thinking about that, too, and I've realized my only drive to leave this place was to get answers." I held up the book. "I have them now. And I made friends here. There's really nothing for me out there. Except maybe some pizza." I grinned at the thought. "Oh, yeah. I'm totally going to pig out while we're in New York."

He chuckled and opened the door to his sporty red car. I looked at mine, parked near the shed.

"Don't worry. It'll be fine. Fenris promised to keep an eye on it," Oanen said.

"You talked to Fenris?"

"Yeah. He called to apologize for his comment last

night. He only meant to defuse the situation so you wouldn't lose your temper with anyone else in the crowd."

"And?"

"And what?"

"Were you okay with his apology?"

"Of course. I knew what he was doing the moment he spoke. That didn't make hearing his words any easier."

I frowned slightly.

"I don't get it."

"I'm trying my hardest not to be jealous because you don't like it. Although I trust you completely, I still don't like other males even looking at you." He leaned down so he could set my bag in the back, putting us face to face. "You're mine, and I never could share well."

His lips brushed mine in a soft kiss. I closed my eyes and threaded my fingers in his hair.

Too quickly, he pulled away and shut the door. I watched him walk around the hood and took those few moments to gather my thoughts. When he opened his door, I was ready.

"So, your possessiveness isn't just a bonding thing?" I asked.

He started the car and gave me a look that started a fire smoldering in my stomach.

"Oh, it's definitely a bonding thing. But, because you asked, I'll keep it in check as best I can."

He backed out of my driveway, and I gave the house one last look. Paint still peeled off the boards, making it look old, but the clean windows and white blanket of snow over the cut grass made it feel less derelict and more cared for.

"We'll be back," Oanen said. "And in the spring, we're painting that thing."

I grinned and turned to watch the road. The familiar, winding path to the barrier only took a few minutes to travel. And when we reached the straight stretch, no scent of burnt hair tickled my nose. However, a tingle ran through my body as we crossed from Uttira into the real world.

I turned my wrist over and looked at the mark of Mantirum.

"It's weird how a little tattoo can make such a big difference."

Oanen chuckled.

"That's what I thought, too, the first time I flew outside."

"So, what's in New York? Other than pain in my ass Paxton?"

"A troll death. The Council wants me to ask around about it."

"Why?"

"Why what?"

"Why you? Why is a troll death a big deal? I mean, we die like humans, right? Well, at least species who don't have books saying the fourth generation needs to knock off the first generation."

"Yes. Most species have human equivalent lifespans. Trolls included. A troll showing up dead isn't a problem. How he died is."

"Well, don't leave me in suspense. Was he eaten? Mutated? Turned inside out? What?"

"You need to stop watching so much TV. The troll died smiling."

I stared at Oanen for a moment, confused. Oanen glanced at me and caught my look.

"You remember Epsid?" he asked.

"Yep."

"That's as happy as trolls get. And that only happens when they're young. As trolls age, they just get ornerier. The troll that died was old. They never smile. That he was still smiling in death is very off."

"Okay. So what would make a troll die with a smile?"

"No idea. That's why we need to check it out."

"And why you?"

He glanced at me.

"Because Uttira has the closest Council, and I'm a cog in training."

"Ugh. I have my mark now. Why not just tell them to shove it?"

"Honestly? I don't mind doing this. It beats getting a job at one of the shops in town to contribute to Uttira."

"Fair enough. What's the plan?"

"See what we can learn from the inglorious patrons of The Goose and Gizzard. According to Adira, it's the best place to gather information. If there is any to gather."

I ignored his mention of Adira, still too annoyed with the woman to even think about her.

"What kind of place is The Goose and Gizzard?"

"Don't know. This will be my first time there."

We passed our first car on the road, and my internal fury gauge only stirred a little, quickly settling with more distance.

"You all right?" Oanen asked. "You got quiet."

"Yeah. I'm okay. I could feel something from that car, but it went away already. Much better than the last time I was in a car in the outside world. The anger used to crawl under my skin and fester there until I wanted to beat someone."

"Let me know if it starts bothering you again, okay?"

"I will."

We talked for the next two hours about what Oanen suspected might have happened to the troll, how I planned to stuff the trunk with enough chocolate to keep Eliana supplied for the next year, and what color we wanted to paint the house.

"I'm still going with rainbow," I said, sticking to the house color of my choice.

"That sounds awful."

"Exactly. It'll work better than a 'keep away' sign on our front lawn," I said with a grin. A sign on the side of the road caught my attention.

"Can we stop at the next gas station? I'm craving some real potato chips."

"Sure." He glanced at me. "Just a snack break, or do you need a break from the traffic?"

The cars we passed so far were all right for the most part. A few made me clench my fists, but again, putting distance between us always brought it back down.

"Just the snack. We already left later than either of us wanted to. It'll be close to midnight by the time we get there the way it is."

"Later is better in this case. Too early, and no one will be at the Gizzard."

He took the next exit and turned into a small gas station.

"What town is this?" I asked as he parked.

"We're just outside of Brunswick, I think."

We both got out of the car, and a tug of tension drew my eyes to a woman at the pump.

"On second thought, fury fire and gas pumps probably aren't a good idea. I think I'm going to stay in the car. Pick something good for me."

I quickly got back inside the car and closed the door. But, sitting there didn't muffle the anger crawling under my skin in the least. So I distracted myself by ogling Oanen's backside as he jogged toward the entrance. The play of muscle under his form fitting t-shirt made me smile.

As soon as he disappeared, though, there was no distraction. How was I going to handle New York if I couldn't even get out of the car at a side-of-the-road gas station? I remembered the rage that consumed me the night Adira introduced me to Eugene in some back alley in the city. It hadn't been pretty. I'd wanted to kill those men. But, that was before I came into my power. Things would be different now. They had to be.

A blast of anger hit me hard. Not the woman who was paying at the pump. Someone else.

I turned my head to look at the car parking two spaces over from me. The driver, a man in his mid-twenties, glanced my way and smiled. The fire inside of me burned hotter. The need to punish clawed at me.

"Don't do it, Megan," I mumbled. "Keep your ass in your seat."

He opened his door.

My hand reached for the handle.

"Weak, Megan. Really weak."

I got out at the same time the man did. His smile widened as I walked his way.

"Hi. Can I help you with something?"

"Don't 'hi' me, asshole. What did you do to piss me off?"

His smile vanished, and he gave me a truly confused look.

"Excuse me?"

People could say the right words and give the right look to make themselves appear good and innocent. But it didn't fool my fury-side. Ever.

"Nice try. Just confess what you did so we can both move on."

His eyes narrowed on me.

"Hot and crazy isn't my type," he said. "Beat it."

He moved to the side as if to walk around me.

"Will Yajlin," I said, stopping him with just my voice. "Confess."

The word brought him to his knees before me. Trembling where he knelt, words tumbled from his mouth. I listened to how he'd just beaten the crap out of his girlfriend before running out for a bag of beef jerky that she didn't want to get for him.

"Beef jerky?"

"I'm not even sure if she's still breathing," he admitted with a sob.

The fire inside of me roared with the truth behind his admission. I could see his girlfriend where she lay, her face bloody and pale. Her chest still.

"Elizabeth is not breathing. She died by your hands."

He mewled pathetically as I grabbed him by his throat and lifted. Fire danced up my arm, slowly consuming my sleeve.

"Will Yajlin, you've earned your place in hell."

With those words, I embraced my fury power. Fire exploded over my skin, and pain ripped through me from my stomach to the top of my head as if I were being split in half.

I opened my mouth and screamed, shattering the windows in Will's car.

The sound of Oanen calling my name was the last thing I heard before the agony of being burned alive swallowed me whole.

# CHAPTER TWO

THE FAINT ECHO OF OANEN SAYING MY NAME AND THE persistent tapping on my cheek made my head throb. I groaned, turned my head, and heaved my guts out.

"Megan, tell me what's wrong?" Oanen said, holding back my hair.

"I'm throwing up," I said, weakly swiping my mouth with the back of my hand.

"Yeah, I can see that. Why, though?"

The gentle stroke of his fingers over my hair took away some of the ache drumming in my skull.

"How am I supposed to know? I just woke up."

The wrongness of that statement struck me as soon as the words left my mouth. I hadn't been sleeping. I'd been in the middle of punishing someone. A guy. No, a murderer.

From my position safely cradled in Oanen's lap, I lifted my head and looked around. We sat in the empty parking space next to our car. The man and his vehicle were gone.

I looked up at Oanen.

"What happened?" I asked.

The worry clouding his gaze intensified.

"I don't know. I came out with your snacks, found you on the ground, and some guy squealing tires out of the parking lot."

"That would have been Will, a guy who just killed his girlfriend. Can you help me up? I need to go to the bathroom and get this taste out of my mouth."

Oanen lifted me to my feet and walked with me to the bathroom. My legs felt a little shaky, and my stomach wasn't sure which way was up. However, none of that bothered me as much as the fact that I'd let a murderer get away.

Oanen said nothing as I closed myself into the dirty washroom. I used the toilet then cleaned up. Skull still pounding, I stared at myself in the mirror and tried to figure out what the hell had happened. I'd obviously done something wrong. But what?

I'd let go of my power just like I had on the beach. Only, the pain had been worse this time. And, instead of feeling better afterward, I hurt. My head. My stomach. Even my back.

Oanen knocked lightly on the door.

"Everything okay?"

"Yeah. Just a minute."

Not wanting to worry him further, I splashed some cool water on my face before opening the door. His concerned gaze swept over me.

"Feeling better?" he asked.

"As well as a girl can after heaving her guts out in front of her boyfriend."

His gaze warmed.

"I like the sound of that."

"You like the sound of me trying to see the inside of my stomach?" I asked in disbelief. "You have issues."

"I like the sound of boyfriend. Not you getting sick; our kind isn't supposed to get sick like that."

"I'd prefer to pretend it didn't happen," I said quickly, noting the pre-lecture look on his face. Which was completely unfair since I hadn't done anything to deserve it.

He lifted my bag. I hadn't noticed him holding it until then.

"In case you wanted to brush," he said.

"You're amazing." I accepted the bag. "And when I come back out, we won't mention my time kissing the pavement ever again."

He nodded, and I closed the door on him once more, relieved that I'd managed to hide just how much my head was hurting. Making a face at myself in the mirror, I slathered my toothbrush with paste and set to work erasing the last few minutes of my life.

While the minty freshness helped quell the remaining queasiness in my stomach, it did nothing to ease my mind. I didn't know what was supposed to happen when I condemned a wicked to hell, but I felt pretty certain that me passing out wasn't it.

I spit and rinsed and considered trying to call my mom again. She'd be able to tell me what went wrong. However, I disregarded that idea as quickly as it formed. Mom had made herself clear during our last call. She had no intention of talking to me until I offed granny dearest. It would be better to wait until I had Mom cornered in New York.

Hopefully, she'd answer questions when we were face to face.

With my brush and paste back in the bag, I opened the door. Oanen turned, pocketing his phone, and I smiled at him.

"What kind of chips did you get me?" I asked, determined to stick to my word and pretend nothing had happened.

He took the bag and walked with me to the car.

"Three different kinds. Sour cream and onion. Cheddar. And vinegar."

"Vinegar?" I asked.

"Something to help balance how sweet you are."

I laughed and gave him a peck on the cheek. Oanen's arms wrapped around my waist, and he held me for a moment. The press of his chest against mine and the feel of his heat seeping through my clothes reminded me that we were going to be staying together tonight. My heart skipped a beat at the thought.

Easing away with a shy smile, I got into the car. The moment my back touched the seat, I winced. Oanen caught my expression and watched me closely as I shifted my position to take the pressure off the area that hurt.

"You're not okay, are you?" he asked.

Gold flecks appeared in his gaze.

"I got knocked into the boat yesterday and hit my back pretty hard. I think it's just bruised."

He frowned slightly.

"I thought you were healed after last night?"

I stared at him for a moment, confused. Although I knew for a fact that the bites on my arms and legs had disappeared after my pyrotechnics display the night before, I couldn't recall if my back had hurt afterward. So much had happened in such a short period of time. Testing my abilities at the Roost. Spending the night in the same bed with Oanen without melting his hair. Getting my mark this morning. So much, in fact, that I'd never stopped to take inventory.

"Yeah, I thought so, too. Maybe when I fell just now, I hurt it again."

"I thought we weren't going to talk about that," he said.

Before I could answer, he leaned in to toss my bag in the backseat and brushed his lips along my neck. I exhaled softly and relaxed against the seat, ignoring the part of my back that stung. When he was done kissing my neck, he lifted his head and studied me.

"I never want to see you on the ground like that again."

"And you think I wanted to be there?" I asked, arching a brow.

His I'll-be-patient-because-you're-not-well expression morphed into his famous pre-lecture expression. I quickly grabbed his head and kissed the hell out of him.

When he finally pulled back, his hair was messy; and I was struggling to breathe and remember my name.

"You won't get away with that every time," he said.

"I might."

His lips twitched.

"You might."

I exhaled in relief when he closed the door. I was crazy about Oanen, but I might threaten his wings again if he attempted to lecture me when I felt this crappy.

My yawn ended with a wince when I shifted sleepily on the seat. Sitting up, I opened my eyes and looked around. The daylight and light traffic had disappeared, replaced by buildings and streetlights as far as I could see.

"Where are we?" I asked.

"The city. We're almost there. How are you feeling?"

I rubbed my face, yawned again, and stretched carefully.

"Better."

"Really?"

He sounded surprised.

"Yes. Really. The headache's gone."

"You had a headache?"

"Just a little one. Sorry I slept so long. I didn't mean to stick you with all the driving."

"It's okay. I figured it would be easier on you if you slept through this part, anyway."

I looked around at all the buildings again and understood what he meant. The streets were crawling with people. However, I didn't even feel a tingle of irritation.

"I'm actually good. No overwhelming urges to hit anyone." I smiled. "See? Powers under control."

"In that case, I'd like to head to the Goose and Gizzard first."

"That's fine with me."

My stomach growled loudly, a reminder of just how empty it was.

"Did you stop somewhere to eat?"

"No. I wanted to wait to see how you felt."

He cast me a pensive side-glance.

"I'm fine. I swear. Whatever happened in the parking lot was because I have no clue what I'm doing. That little book my mom left me is far from an instruction manual. While you ask questions about your dead troll, I plan to ask about a fury."

"Good. I'm struggling not to be worried, and I'll feel a lot better if your mom can clarify her comment about you suffering the longer you wait."

He pulled over in front of one of the many tall buildings on the block.

"We're about eight blocks north of Central Park," he said. "We're staying near the park on the west side. My parents have a condo there with roof access. I texted you the address already."

"Okay," I said, drawing out the word. "Why are you telling me this?"

He shut off the engine and turned to look at me.

"We're in a city full of people, going into a bar full of creatures. The likelihood of you running into someone punishable for their wickedness isn't just high; it's definite. If you end up chasing someone down when I'm not looking, I want to know that you can find your way back to me."

I reached up and set my hand over his tense jaw muscle.

"I should tell you not to worry about me, but honestly, I like it. I haven't had someone worry like this in a very long time. Thank you."

He turned his head to kiss the palm of my hand.

"Let's get this done so we can go relax at the condo."

The way he said it made my stomach dip and spin in a

mix of anticipation and nerves. I quickly exited the car so he wouldn't see either in my expression.

Looking at the plain building before me, I frowned. The brick and stone façade screamed apartment for rent, not supernatural bar.

"I thought we were going to the Goose and Gizzard."

"We are."

He threaded his fingers through mine as he joined me on the sidewalk. With a light tug on my hand, he led me up the stairs toward the door.

A tingle of something brushed my skin and made the hair on my arms stand up when we reached the landing.

"Magic," Oanen said softly. "Keeps the humans out."

He opened the door, and a low murmur of voices filled the air as we stepped into the large bar.

The Goose and Gizzard wasn't anything like the Roost. No music with a dancing beat blared from speakers. No nice couches waited for intimate moments. No color. No fun. Probably because the patrons of the Goose and Gizzard edged toward geriatric rather than teen.

A bar ran the back length of the place. Several pool tables lined the right side with booths toward the front. To the left, there were a couple of battered tables where a few creatures were eating their meals. The place looked like a complete dive. Definitely not the kind of establishment I could see my mom frequenting. However, the troll snoring on the pool table to our right told me this was just the place Oanen needed to be.

He studied the troll for a moment then met my gaze.

"Good luck," he said.

"Yeah, you too. I'm going to go talk to the bartender."

He nodded and stepped toward the sleeping creature.

I strode to the bar. Behind me, the snoring stopped, and I glanced back at Oanen. With his arms crossed and his expression masked, he stood beside the irate troll.

"Go away," the troll rumbled.

"No. You and I need to talk."

The troll drew back his fist and made to hit Oanen. Oanen caught the extra-large, meaty fist in his own. The contact echoed in the room and quieted the low murmur of conversation.

"I have no quarrel with you," Oanen said clearly. "Just some questions that need to be answered."

Someone snorted behind me, drawing my attention back to the bar. The few patrons who sat there appeared older. Greying hair. Stooped shoulders. Expressions in varying degrees of life-bitterness.

"Just what we need," a craggy-faced man said.

I took the empty seat beside the man. With his leather jacket and weathered face, he looked like an old biker.

"What do you mean?" I asked.

"An enforcer. We have no freedom the way it is. What's left to suppress?"

"What's an enforcer?" I asked.

He gave me an incredulous look.

"The ones responsible for the current state of our world."

"You think that guy's going to suppress you in some way?" I asked, trying a different approach.

"They all do. First, it was don't eat humans. Now, it's don't kill humans. Stay hidden. Stay quiet. I miss the days when I could open my wings and soar high. If humans scurried below me like frightened cattle, I could scorch them or not. It was my choice back then."

The person on the biker's right said something I couldn't hear, and the biker chuckled.

"You are right, my friend. This world is no longer ours. The enforcers have made sure we have no place in it."

I looked in the mirror behind the bar and saw that the person on the biker's right was hidden by a deep hood. Only the bottom half of the man's face was visible, showing his whiskered chin wasn't salted with grey like the biker's.

"What can I get you?" the bartender asked, coming my way.

"A glass of water and a menu."

He belly-laughed and walked away.

"I don't get it," I said.

"Fledgling," the biker beside me said, "the stuff they make here isn't meant for a menu."

I frowned and glanced back at the other patrons who were quietly eating. Oanen had his back to me, in quiet conversation with the troll. If the scowl on the troll's face was any indication of their conversation, I didn't imagine things were going well for Oanen.

The bartender walked out of a side door and delivered a plate of mashed up food to one of the tables in the main room. I couldn't identify what exactly was on the plate. But, the chunks were a bit too large for stew.

I sniffed the air and watched the patron take his first enthusiastic bite. It smelled like normal food in the Goose and Gizzard, but I couldn't forget what kind of creatures this place catered to.

"It's not human, is it?" I asked, glancing at the biker. "The food."

The guy's hard gaze locked with mine.

"Are you a special kind of stupid to ask something like that with an enforcer in the same room?"

"Apparently."

"We don't serve human here," the bartender said, having returned with a glass of water and a plate of food. The glass he slammed in front of me, and the burger with fries he set down in front of the guy beside me.

"Sorry," I said holding up my hands. "I didn't know any of us existed until a few months ago. Blame my ignorance on my parenting."

"See?" the biker said, looking at the bartender. "This is what I'm talking about." He focused on me once more. "We need to return to the old ways. You would have known what you were from the moment you were born. You wouldn't have had your powers suppressed or grown in the shadows of a world you were made to dominate." He closed his eyes, and a shudder ran through him. When he opened his eyes again, I stared at the vertical slits of his pupils that reminded me far too much of Lucia.

The biker shrugged out of his jacket and something heavy fell from his back. He shook himself again, and the thick leather of his wings unfurled further. I'd read about his species in a book. Dragon.

"My kind used to rule the skies," he said. "Now, I hide in a hovel of broken buildings on a forgotten island. Where's the pride and majesty in that?"

I didn't know what to say.

"If you're smart, you'll stay away from enforcers," the

dragon continued, tilting his head toward Oanen. "You might actually find a few moments in life where you can enjoy being what you were meant to be."

The cloaked figure stood and clapped the dragon on his back.

"Only the lucky can fulfill their true purpose," he said before making his way toward the side door the bartender had used.

"Very true," the bartender said. He took the money from the guy's spot and started to move away.

"Wait. There's a fury here in the city. Do either of you know where I can find her?"

The bartender started to laugh, and the dragon swore.

"I'm done with this place." The dragon threw down some cash and stood. His gaze pinned me as he put on his jacket and hid his wings.

"If you had any brains, you wouldn't be in here asking for that kind of trouble."

He stalked out of the bar.

"You should listen to him," the bartender said. "Furies are nasty business. Not just for humans. Don't involve yourself with them, or you'll find yourself with a one-way ticket to hell."

He reached for the dragon's untouched plate of food.

"Hold on," I said, stopping him. "What is that?"

"A bacon cheeseburger. The best you'll find in Harlem."

"The dragon paid for it, right?"

"Yeah, so what?"

I grabbed the plate and pulled it toward me.

"He knew bacon cheeseburger was my favorite." I picked up the burger and took a large bite before the bartender could take it from me. The bacony goodness hit my taste buds with love, and I groaned.

"So good," I said around a mouthful of burger.

The bartender shook his head and walked away. I swallowed my first bite and took a second one. Burgers in Uttira had been okay. The lean meat and limited topping choices stunted the flavor possibilities, though. Unlike this burger. Grease and mayonnaise dripped onto the plate as I held the concoction, ready for my next mouthful.

I turned it slightly to look at the wadded stack of bacon, onion rings, lettuce and tomato on top of the inch and a half thick patty. There had to be seven pieces of bacon. I swallowed, grinned, and took another mouthful.

As I chewed, the room gave a weird spin.

Frowning, I shook my head slightly. My blink felt heavy, too. The background noise faded, and movement slowed. I breathed sluggishly. Something was wrong. Why wasn't I concerned? I knew I should be. It felt like when Eliana touched me to syphon my anger. Only, no one was touching me.

I swallowed my bite and looked down at the burger. A grey-green powder dusted the bacon.

A darkness swam into the room, rapidly tunneling my vision. I opened my mouth to call Oanen's name, but nothing came out. The bar and the people sitting beside me disappeared.

The last thing I saw was the burger falling to my plate.

# CHAPTER THREE



"JUST GET RID OF HER BEFORE THE SPELL WEARS OFF."

The words poked at my mind in the persistently annoying way of a mosquito until the echo of fading footsteps took the place of the words.

My brain didn't want to work. Neither did my eyes.

I wanted to sink back into the fog shrouding my thoughts, but some small part of me insisted I resist the pull. I groaned, my head lolling to the side.

A small laugh teased my ears.

"The spell's already wearing off. You're in trouble."

The sharp rattle of metal and a high-pitched shriek annoyed me enough that I managed to open my eyes. Bits of my surroundings swam in and out of focus with each slow blink.

A cement floor. A table with a cage on it, not far away and to my right. A bald kid walking toward me. Sharp teeth.

I jerked back and tried to lift my hand to rub my eyes. My arm wouldn't move.

I opened my eyes again and stared at the glowing ropes tying me to a sturdy chair. The cloud of my exhale momentarily distracted me as I gave another tug. The ropes tightened around my forearms, biting into the skin. It should have hurt, but I was too cold to feel anything.

"Struggling only makes it worse."

Lifting my gaze, I found the child-sized creature standing within kicking distance, which I would have tried to do if my ankles hadn't been bound, too.

He studied me as I studied him. His size was the only thing he had in common with a human kid. The wizened wrinkles creasing his face and the tuft of hair sticking out from his pointed ears matched perfectly with his rough-spun shirt that looked a hundred years old.

"You're in a pickle, aren't you, my pretty plaything. Old Elbner will set things right. For a price."

"This is really not the way to make a good impression with me," I said, my voice surprisingly clear. "Untie me now."

"I can't. Once those bonds are on, only the buyer can untie you. Prevents backcrossing on deals struck."

"He's lying," a high-pitched voice chirped.

I looked beyond good 'ol Elbner to the cage on the table. A small creature with wings flitted around, shaking the bars as if testing their strength. When the thing saw I was looking at it, it flew at the bars and stared at me in return. A tiny shirt hung loosely from its bony shoulders, and the long pants it wore were held up with a string belt.

"You're pretty," it said.

"Thank you. What are you?"

"A brownie."

Elbner stepped in my line of sight.

"We can share his wings if you'd like." He licked his lips, the glisten making me feel sick.

The brownie squealed, and I scowled at Elbner.

"He looks pretty attached to his wings. Now, are you going to untie me or what?"

"I told you. Can't."

"He's lying," the brownie called again.

Elbner growled and pivoted to the cage, which made the brownie squeal and take off. It zoomed around it's prison in a panic, trying to find a way out.

"How is he lying?" I asked.

"His master told him to get rid of you. He's supposed to set you free."

Elbner stopped advancing toward the cage and cast a sly look over his shoulder at me.

"'Get rid of' doesn't mean set free," he said.

"Someone bigger than you briefly considered killing me," I said. "She decided not to risk it, though."

He turned toward me fully, a low chuckle rising from him.

"Oh? And what stopped her? Fear of you?"

He moved closer and reached out a bony finger, trailing it from my chin down my throat. The sharp edge of his nail scraped my skin, not quite breaking it but definitely leaving a mark.

A spark of anger lit inside of me. Small in comparison to what I'd felt in the past, but enough. I tugged hard on the bonds. They bit in painfully, and I pulled harder still. The fire inside me burned brighter with the pain.

"Fear of pissing off the gods," I said.

Elbner stopped touching me and stared at me with a puzzled frown.

"What are you?" he asked.

"You tell me, and I'll tell you."

"I'm a goblin."

I closed my eyes and focused on the fire burning inside of me. When I opened my eyes again, an orange glow reflected on Elbner's skin.

"I'm a fury."

The old creature's eyes rounded. He made a choked sound and stumbled back a few steps as the ropes binding me began to smolder. The glow faded, and the ropes fell away in seconds.

I stood, and the old guy fell to his knees in a shaking heap.

"Looks like you're in a pickle, aren't you?" the brownie chirped happily from his cage.

"I never meant to hurt you," the goblin said, his voice muffled. "It was only a prank. Just my nature. To trick and tease."

"And the brownie wings? Is that tempting offer still open?"

The brownie looked at me in horror as Elbner jumped up and raced over to the table.

"Yes. Of course. Two might be a bit filling, but I'd be happy to eat the second one for you." He pulled a rusted knife from the back of his ripped pants.

The fire, which had freed me, slowly died. How could wanting to cut the wings off that tiny creature not be wicked?

Annoyed, I reached Elbner before he could open the

cage. The old goblin made an awful moaning sound when I grabbed his arm and spun him around. The useless knife went clattering to the floor.

"I'm not interested in his wings. I said that to see what kind of person you are. And, I have my answer. Not a good one."

He started to frantically shake his head.

"I'm no enforcer, but I'm not wicked. Just a few pranks. Harmless tricks."

"Right now, I don't care what you've done in the past; I'm interested in how I got here and why. Start talking."

"My master only wants—"

His words stopped, but his lips still moved. I wanted to swear.

"What *can* you tell me?" I asked, interrupting his silent confession.

He licked his lips nervously as his gaze shifted around the room. Suddenly, his expression brightened.

"I can serve you," he said. "You can be my master if you'll have me."

"Ew. No." The last thing I wanted was this creepy old goblin hanging around me.

"Say, yes," the brownie said. "The spell will fade once his ownership changes hands. He'll be able to give you answers eventually."

I looked at the brownie.

"You're just full of information. If I let you out, is something bad going to happen?"

The little creature giggled and pointed at Elbner.

"I'll pull out his ear hair."

Elbner growled. "Touch me, and I'll eat your wings."

"No, you won't," I said. I reached for the cage door. "What does being his master mean?" I asked.

"He has to listen to you," the brownie answered earnestly. "And, if you treat him well, he'll listen. If you don't treat him well, he'll make your life miserable then leave."

My hand hesitated on the latch.

"Treat him well? What's that mean, exactly?"

"Feed him. Goblins like milk. Milk soaked oats. Milk soaked oats with honey are their favorite."

"Not true," Elbner said. "Milk soaked oats with honey and brownie wings are my favorite."

"Why are you so willing to trade masters?" I asked, ignoring his obsession with the brownie's wings.

"His master forgot to feed him today."

The phone in my pocket buzzed.

"It's been doing that a lot," Elbner said. "I like the sound. Reminds me of wings beating."

I pulled out my phone and looked at a string of messages from Oanen, the oldest from over three hours ago. The first one started out calm enough, asking where I'd gone. Then, each one after progressively showed his growing concern. The final one worried me.

*If I don't hear from you in ten minutes, I'm calling Adira.*

I typed out a quick message while keeping an eye on Elbner.

*I'm okay. I'll call in a minute. Are brownies and goblins safe to be around?*

His reply was immediate.

*Safe enough. Where are you?*

I looked at Elbner.

"Fine. I'll be your master. As soon as the spell wears off, you're going to tell me what's going on here. Got it?"

He nodded.

"And no eating brownie wings while I'm your master. I'll feed you everything else but that."

He scowled at me and gave a single nod.

I opened the brownie's cage and squealed when the thing flew straight at my face. Its tiny arms stuck to my neck as it hugged me.

"Thank you! Thank you! I thought I would die in that cage like my grandparents." He released me and flitted back to look me in the eyes.

"My name is Piepen. What's yours?"

"Pie Pen?"

He nodded.

"I'm Megan."

He flew forward and hugged me again. His little hand stroked the side of my neck.

"I love you, Megan." The tiny puff of his breath brushed my skin. Or was that his lips? Were his hips moving?

"Okay. I think I'm all hugged out."

He didn't let go. I carefully pinched his shirt and tugged him loose.

"You're free to go, now," I said.

His happy face fell.

"Go? I have nowhere to go. My grandparents are dead now, and I have no parents. Please don't leave me behind." His small cherub face scrunched up, and tears glistened in his eyes.

"Let's talk about this later. I really need to make a phone call."

With numb fingers, I dialed Oanen. He picked up immediately.

"Megan, where are you?"

"Oh, um…" I looked around at the empty room. "I think I'm in some kind of old warehouse."

The phone was quiet for a long moment.

"I want an address, not a description." The warning in his tone made me grin.

"Hold on." I looked at Elbner. "What's the address for this place?"

He opened his mouth, but nothing came out. I wished I was a lip reader.

"Fine. Where's the exit?"

Elbner led the way to a set of stairs. I clumsily jogged down the first flight with Piepen flitting alongside of me, his tiny wings buzzing.

"What's that noise?" Oanen asked as I started down the second flight.

"That's Piepen, a brownie I set free."

"And you won't regret it," Piepen said. "I'm good at making beds and washing dishes."

"You're going to regret it," Oanen said in my ear.

"Already am," I said softly.

I pushed through the door at the bottom of the stairwell and stepped into what looked like a shipping yard. Metal containers and boards poked through the snow and littered the space before the building.

"There's a sign to the right," Elbner said.

Glancing back, I caught the glint of his eyes as he hovered in the shadows. He pointed down the road.

"Just a second, Oanen. I need to run to the street corner."

He remained quiet as I jogged.

"26$^{th}$ and 4$^{th}$ street," I said, looking at the signs.

"There is no 26$^{th}$ and 4$^{th}$ street in Harlem, Megan. Open the map on your phone."

I put him on speaker, pulled the map up on my phone, and sent him my current location.

"You're not even in Manhattan. How did you get across the river?"

I looked around and saw the glimmer of lights reflecting on water further down the street. A shiver coursed through me. How in the hell had I crossed that?

"Not sure," I said. "I just woke up fifteen minutes ago."

"Woke up?"

"Yeah, I think the burger I ate was drugged."

A shiver of emotion tingled along the back of my neck. Anger. Fear. A lot of fear.

"Are you safe? Right now. Are you safe?" he demanded.

"Oanen? Did you just..." The idea that I'd just felt what he was feeling made my stomach dip and my heart flutter.

"Just what?" he asked.

"Nothing. I'm safe."

"I'm flying to you."

The call disconnected, and I frowned at the phone.

"I don't like him," Piepen said. "He didn't sound nice."

"He's really nice. And, I like him a lot."

A scruff of noise from behind us had Piepen diving for my hair. I turned, trying to ignore the brownie shaking on my shoulder.

"Lost, honey?" a man asked, stepping from the shadows.

"No. Just waiting for my boyfriend."

"Want me to keep you company?"

"Thanks, but I don't think that'll help his mood."

A snarl came from behind the man a moment before a long piece of two by four lumber swung out of the dark. The chunk of wood hit the man in the head. His eyes rolled back, and he fell like a brick to reveal Elbner standing behind him.

"What the hell, Elbner? Why did you hit him?"

"He was going to hurt you."

"No, he wasn't. I'm a fury, remember? I would have felt his wickedness if he was going to do something."

Elbner cast the board aside and scowled at me.

"If you mistreat him, he'll make you miserable," Piepen said softly, right in my ear. "He'll want extra milk for protecting you." I was about to thank the brownie for the reminder when something touched my earlobe. Something tiny and wet. I shuddered and reached for Piepen.

"Okay. Ride's over. Get out of my hair."

The little guy flew out and went to investigate the fallen man.

My phone rang again, and I quickly lifted it, ready to ask Oanen to hurry up. Instead of Oanen's name, Eliana's flashed. I smiled and answered.

"You officially broke your promise," she said.

"Huh?"

"It's after midnight. You said you would check in daily, and I didn't get a call yesterday."

"The day I left doesn't count."

"Sure, start bending the rules already. So, what's it like having freedom?"

I watched Piepen lift the guy's eyelid.

"Knock it off," I said.

"Do I even want to know what Oanen's doing?" Eliana asked.

"Not Oanen. A brownie named Piepen is messing around with some guy's eye."

Piepen zipped over to me and flitted around my head, trying to listen. I waved my hand, shooing him away.

"A brownie?" Eliana asked.

"Yeah, long story."

"I've got time."

"I let him out of a cage, and now he's following me."

"I'm not following. I'm going to help you. I'll take care of your house."

"No, you won't," Elbner said from the shadows. "That's my job."

"No, you take care of everything outside. I take care of the inside."

Eliana started snickering.

"Two of them? What are you going to do with two?" she asked.

"One's a brownie and one's a goblin. And I have no idea." I paced to the corner and back toward the shadows where the man lay, still unconscious, before turning again. Moving wasn't warming me up like I'd hoped.

"They're not going to like the hotel or the car. They're much happier in real homes," Eliana said.

"She sounds nice," Piepen said. "I like her."

"Aw! Isn't he sweet," she said.

Piepen's face lit up with joy, and he started zipping around my head faster.

"Stop. He can hear you, and I think you're going to give him a heart attack. What's wrong with hotels?"

"What's a hotel?" Piepen asked, slowing to hover in front of me.

Elbner stepped from the shadows, a severe scowl on his face.

"A hotel? A hotel!" His ears quivered with his anger. "I will not lower myself to the upkeep of rented rooms."

"Told you," Eliana said in my ear.

"I have a house," I assured Elbner. "I'm just visiting the city for a while."

"Where's your house?" he demanded. "I'll wait for you there."

"Tell him," Eliana encouraged through the phone. "You'll be happier with him here. I'll feed them both for you."

"Are you sure?" I asked her.

"Yep. It'll be fine."

I looked at both of the creatures, hoping I wasn't about to make a mistake.

"I live in Uttira. N125 W837 Crooked Road."

"Hmm." Elbner looked north. "It'll take me a few days," he said after a moment. "It better not be a nice house."

"Oh, it's not," I assured him.

"Tell him I'll have a bowl of honey-soaked oats waiting for him," Eliana said.

Elbner's eyes gleamed, and I knew he'd heard her.

"Can I go, too? Can I?" Piepen begged.

A speculative look glazed over Elbner's eyes as the old goblin stared at Piepen's wings.

"Can I trust you to care for Piepen?" I asked Elbner. "That means protecting him and his wings, from yourself and everyone else."

Elbner grumped and grumbled before nodding. He waved for Piepen and started across the street. The brownie-boy flew at my head, kissed the tip of my nose, then took off into the dark after Elbner. Once they were far enough away, I gave Eliana the rundown about what had happened once we got to New York. Getting drugged. Waking in the warehouse. A goblin with answers but bound by a spell.

"I'll call you if he says anything about who his previous master was," Eliana said when I finished.

"Thank you. And watch yourself around both of them. Oanen said they wouldn't hurt me, but Elbner seems sketchy."

"Did he make you mad?" she asked.

"Surprisingly, no."

"Then I'm sure he'll be fine."

An eagle's cry split the air.

"I better go," I said. "Oanen's coming, and I need to check the guy Elbner knocked out."

"What guy?"

"I'll tell you later."

I hung up and hurried over to the man on the ground. When I tapped his cheek, he groaned, a sign he was close to coming to. At least, I hoped so.

Straightening, I stepped away from him and looked to the sky. The clouds and the nearby streetlights made it impossible to see Oanen until he fell from the sky. His graceful shift from griffin to human as he landed made my pulse quicken. I doubted I would ever tire of watching him do that.

He strode toward me, his golden gaze locked on my face. The tick of his jaw and the scowl on his face distracted me from the fact he was walking around naked in New York in the middle of winter as if it was no big deal.

Without a word, Oanen pulled me into his arms and held me tight. I could feel him shaking and tried to hold back my wince when his hand brushed over the sore spot on my back. Wrapping my arms around his waist, I just let him hold me.

"Fury's aren't the only ones with a temper," he said against my hair. "Don't ever leave my side again, Megan. New York wouldn't survive what I would do to find you."

The man behind me groaned. Oanen lifted his head, and I pulled back in time to see his pupils dilate. I quickly cupped Oanen's face and forced his attention on me.

"I'm tired, cold, and a little sore. Feel like giving me a ride home, bird boy?"

The heated look he gave me sent a shiver all the way to my toes.

"I'm never letting you go again, Megan. I'm done playing nice."

## CHAPTER FOUR

MY STOMACH DIPPED TO MY TOES.

"What do you mean?" I asked.

He stepped back and shifted to his feathers without answering. When I didn't immediately move, he swung his head toward me and snapped his beak.

With his words still ringing in my ears, I hustled to climb aboard the Oanen Express. Loose snow from the sidewalks swirled around us as he started to beat his wings. Steadily, he rose into the air. I leaned forward and wrapped my arms around his neck, snuggling into his heat. Even with my jacket on, I felt the sting of the occasional snow flake drifting in the air.

Looking below, I watched the expanse of the river pass by. Awe filled me when I lifted my eyes from the water to the skyline. Lights stretched as far as I could see.

"It's so pretty," I said, smoothing my hand over the feathers at his neck.

We passed over buildings, climbing higher and higher. I

shivered slightly, and my fingers grew stiff. Not that I really noticed. I was staring at everything. The tiny cars moving far below. Our reflection in the glass of buildings so tall, I'd get bored trying to count the floors. When we hit the park, I knew we were getting close to the condo he'd mentioned.

Again, his words came back to me. How had he been playing nice, and what was going to change? Ugh. Did that mean I was in for lectures now?

I was still debating what he'd meant and how I might avoid any form of conflict that would tick me off when he started to descend toward a rooftop with a lit-up, glass sunroom. The balcony had been cleared of snow, so nothing swirled around us as he landed.

Sliding off his back, I looked at the cute table and chairs just inside the glass.

"Come on."

Oanen grabbed my hand and pulled me toward the door.

"Are you mad?" I asked, scrambling to follow him. "Because, if you are, I don't think we should go inside."

"You're freezing. We're going inside."

I let out a long, heavy exhale and said nothing as he dragged me through the sunroom into a modern kitchen. He didn't stop there. When I saw he was pulling me toward a living room with pale grey stained hardwood floors, I balked.

"At least, let me take off my shoes," I said, trying to tug my hand free.

Instead of letting go, he turned and scooped me into his arms.

"Shoes aren't a problem now."

With my eyes wide, I stared at his determined expression. The look on his face worried me. I set my hand on his chest and felt him flinch. My chest tightened with apprehension.

"I don't want to fight," I said quietly. "I don't want to lose my temper again. Not with you."

His gaze dipped to me before returning to the hall he walked.

"We're not going to fight because you're going to listen."

I struggled with the initial urge to bristle at those words by chanting, "I will not fry my boyfriend," in my head.

When he turned into a bedroom, my pulse spiked, and butterflies launched for flight in my stomach.

"Um, what are you doing?" I asked.

He set me on my feet and stared down at me, his eyes still amber.

"You can warm up two ways. Shower or me."

My mouth dropped open for a moment.

"Is that an invitation?" he asked.

I snapped my mouth shut and crossed my arms. He was right. He wasn't playing nice anymore. And I wasn't amused.

"Where's the bathroom?" I asked.

He pointed to the right.

Narrowing my eyes at him, I started to turn that direction. I didn't make it a step before he grabbed my arms and pulled me to his chest. My heart skipped a beat. Gazes locked, we stared at each other for a moment. Oh-so-slowly, he lowered his head. My breath caught, and the frantic beat of my heart echoed in my ears.

"I think you're choosing the wrong door," he whispered just before his lips settled onto mine.

He held me close, his mouth claiming me in a way that sent a buzz of need rushing through every limb. Desperate for an anchor, I gripped his arms and groaned at the onslaught. His hands moved from my arms to encircle my waist, the move pressing his hips to mine and making his need for me impossible to ignore.

The angle of the kiss changed, becoming all consuming. His hand slid under my shirt and up my side, his fingers skimming the sensitive skin over my ribs. All my focus was on that hand until his other hand touched the damaged spot on my back.

I pulled back with a gasp and blinked up at him, disoriented, and panting for air.

"Oanen, wait."

"I am. But, I don't need to do it patiently."

He grabbed the back of my head and kissed me hard. My lips tingled when he finally eased away.

"Get in the shower and start talking. I want to know what the hell happened tonight."

His bossy attitude cut through the haze of passion he'd created.

"I want 'playing nice' Oanen back."

"I want you in that bed. One of us might get what they want tonight."

I retreated a step toward the bathroom, and Oanen shadowed the move.

"Cut it out, Oanen," I warned, taking another step.

"You're mad," he said as he matched my movement. "And you're afraid."

"I am not."

He shook his head slowly, not closing the distance between us, not giving me any more space, either.

"You're not afraid of me but yourself. Of what you want."

Stepping into the bathroom, I gripped the door then slammed it shut.

"Talk, Megan," he said from just outside. "Or I come in."

"There's not much to say. I was sitting at the bar one minute, and the next, I was waking up and finding out I was tied to a chair. All I remember from the bar is a dragon who got upset when he heard there was a fury in town—not me, my mom—and left."

I turned on the water to warm.

"I was starving, so I stole the burger he didn't even touch. There was this powder on the bacon. It didn't taste funny, and I didn't notice it until I was four bites in."

As I spoke, I stripped out of my clothes, taking care with my shirt. As much as I twisted in the mirror, I couldn't quite see the spot that hurt.

"When I came to, I realized I was inside that warehouse with a goblin who couldn't tell me anything about why I was there or how I'd arrived. He was spelled too, you know? Like the library prevented me from talking about anything."

I stepped into the shower.

"I called you as soon as I saw the messages. You hung up on me. The goblin knocked out the guy on the street for talking to me. Then Eliana called and said I should send the goblin and the brownie to Uttira and that she'd call when the spell wore off the goblin."

I spun under the water, wincing at the sting on my back. I must have scraped it when I fell in the parking lot.

"That's everything?" he asked, not sounding as muffled as he should.

Knowing that he was in the bathroom with me while I was completely naked had me flushing from head to toe.

"Everything I can remember. What about you? What happened with the troll?" I asked, hoping to distract him from hearing my racing pulse.

"I'll tell you when you're done." The door clicked shut.

I rolled my eyes and quickly washed. When I finished, I opened the curtain and found a tank top with matching character shorts and a clean pair of underwear waiting. My old clothes were gone.

I dried off, not sure how I felt about that. A guy who's willing to pick up? Not a bad thing. A guy who's laying out what I should wear next? Possibly more controlling than I could accept. Yet, those were the only pajamas I'd packed, so was it really controlling or just common sense that those would be the clothes I'd want?

With my hair wrapped in the towel, I dressed and opened the door. Oanen was waiting just outside. His steady gaze swept over me, and I was relieved to see blue instead of gold.

"The troll?" I said, taking the towel from my head and hanging it on the back of the door.

"The troll in the bar knew the one who'd died but had no idea who would have killed him or why."

"So, no leads?"

"No. The dead troll was old, his family already gone. Typical of his age, he had few friends and kept to himself.

His only socialization was going to the Gizzard once a week for a beer and a burger."

I made a face when he said burger.

"We need to figure out what was on that bacon," I said.

"Agreed. But in the morning. You're pale, and you look tired."

He held out his hand. I looked at it, then the bed in the only bedroom in this place. My pulse picked up again.

"You know I won't force anything," he said softly.

"I know." But I wasn't sure I'd want to stop if he kissed me again like he had before.

Instead of taking his hand, I turned away and took a step toward the bed without him.

"Megan."

The anger in that word surprised me, and I looked back at him. His gaze wasn't on my face but on my back. He took two steps forward and pulled the back of my shirt up.

"Hey!"

"Is this what happened?" he demanded.

"What? I don't know what you're talking about."

His finger traced around the area that hurt.

"Is it bruised?" I asked.

"No. It's a raw sore. Like a burn."

"I wasn't near anything hot, so I doubt it's a burn. And it hurt before I was drugged, so I don't think anything happened when I was sleeping. Maybe I scraped myself when I fell," I said, repeating my earlier theory.

"Hold your shirt. Let me get something for it."

I held my shirt up while he dabbed a cooling ointment on the wound and bandaged it to keep my shirt from scabbing to it. I could feel his anger and agitation; I felt pretty certain it wasn't directed at me, though.

When he finished doctoring me, he led me to the bed and pulled back the covers.

"Go to sleep, Megan."

Once again, gold was filling his stoic gaze. I quickly got into bed.

SUNLIGHT BATHED my face and seared through my eyelids.

I groaned and pulled the covers over my head. Behind me, Oanen chuckled. The arm around my waist tightened, bringing my back flush with his warm, bare chest. His fingers moved under my shirt, stroking my belly, which growled.

"It's too early," I mumbled as if he'd just told me to get out of bed.

"It's almost noon." His lips brushed the back of my neck.

I shivered, and my eyes popped open when his fingers stroked my skin more firmly.

"All right, I'm up." I scrambled out of bed and raced for the bathroom.

He left me alone while I slowly went through my morning routine. When I reemerged minty fresh, my bag waited on the made bed. The bedroom door was closed, and I was alone.

I quickly got dressed and found him waiting in the kitchen, talking on the phone. His serious expression and the way he tracked my progress made me nervous.

"That confirms the first death was part of something. We'll check it out."

He hung up and pocketed the phone.

"Another troll," he said without me asking. "He was found not far from where you were last night. Dead with a smile on his face, just like the first one. We need to identify him and ask around again."

"Does the Council have any ideas about what's happening?"

"No. That's why we're here."

"So, look at a dead troll then back to the Gizzard?"

"Yeah. Want to risk something to eat, first? I don't want another burger to tempt you."

I made a face.

"I doubt anything from the Gizzard will tempt me ever again."

I followed him to the double doors and stepped into a hallway where he pushed the button to call the elevator.

"No flying today?" I asked.

"No. You were too cold last night. We'll drive."

The trip down was quiet. When we stepped out into a modern, plush lobby area, I spotted Oanen's car through the glass doors.

I shivered when I stepped outside, and it had nothing to do with the temperature. In the daylight, I could feel wisps of mild wickedness around me.

"That's weird," I said as Oanen opened the passenger door for me.

"What is?"

"I feel more wickedness during the day than at night. I thought it would have been the other way around."

He frowned and looked around.

"Me too."

I shrugged and got in then started buckling my seatbelt while he closed the door and walked around the car.

"I asked Adira if she knew where we could find your mom," he said as he slid behind the wheel.

"Oh? How'd that work out for you?"

"As well as you're imagining. She said for your safety, we should not seek her out." Oanen didn't sound pleased with that answer.

"Yeah, I got the same reaction from the old dragon last night when I asked if he'd heard about a fury."

"Do you want to try calling her again?" he asked, merging into traffic.

"No. I'll find her. It just might take a while." My stomach growled again. "Think we can still find breakfast somewhere?"

"There's a diner not far from here that my dad recommended. They serve breakfast all day."

The diner, only a few blocks away, was tucked in the lower level of a large building, just like every other business in the area. The light scent of breakfast foods teased my nose as soon as I got out of the car. My mouth watered.

Within minutes, we were seated at a table, sipping juice and waiting for our food.

"While I was talking to the dragon last night, he called you an enforcer. What does that mean?"

"When you work for any of the councils, your role is technically to enforce the Mantirum laws."

"He also said you're suppressing their rights.

Apparently, he wants to be able to toast some humans if it strikes his fancy."

"Some of the old-timers are still having a hard time adapting to the laws created over five hundred years ago."

"Holy crap. He was that old?"

"Probably a little older," Oanen said.

"Wow. How old is your dad?"

"In his sixties. Mom's a lot older."

His dad didn't look nearly that old. Late thirties, maybe. Just like his mom. I itched to ask more but didn't want to be overheard.

"I don't really know how old my mom is," I said.

He reached out and placed his hand over mine.

"It's nothing you need to worry about now. I talked to Eliana last night after you fell asleep. I let her know how important it is to find out what happened once your visitors arrive."

"Oh no. What did you tell her? I didn't go into detail because I didn't want her to worry."

"I told her the truth. Someone tried taking you from me."

I tugged my hand from his and scowled at him.

"Eliana's probably freaking out now, thinking I'm in danger."

"No. She's going to try to figure out if there's a way to get your friend to talk sooner."

The waitress came with our food, distracting me from my annoyance. The stack of pancakes on my "side" plate made my mouth water just as much as the over-easy eggs, hash browns, and sausage.

It wasn't until I stuffed the last bite of syrup-soaked pancakes into my mouth that my thoughts circled back to our conversation. No matter what Oanen said, Eliana would worry. That's just who she was. I needed to prove to her and Oanen that I was fine, and the only way to do that was to prove no one intentionally drugged me.

"The burger wasn't even meant for me."

Oanen studied me from across the table, an amused light in his eyes.

"Do you want more?" he asked.

I looked down at my empty plates.

"I don't think I could eat another bite."

"Then why are you talking about burgers?"

I leaned forward and lowered my voice.

"Last night. I took the burger the dragon ordered because he'd left without touching it. I don't think anyone was trying to drug me. I think someone was trying to drug the dragon. Whoever the—Elbner's friend was, he told Elbner to let me go. Why drug me and let me go if I was the intended target?"

"Why drug a dragon?" Oanen said with a thoughtful frown. He reached for his wallet. "We need to get back to the Gizzard."

"I thought we were going to check out the warehouse first."

"You sure your stomach's up for it?"

"Please. I never get sick."

He frowned at me.

"We agreed to pretend that never happened," I said.

He exhaled heavily, placed some money on the table,

stood, then held out his hand. I slipped my fingers through his and followed him out the door. A new tingle of annoyance traced down my spine and pulled my attention to a man in a business suit, crossing the street.

I took a step in that direction, and Oanen's hold on my hand tightened. I turned back to him with a scowl, ready to tell him to let go.

The sight of his hard, golden gaze killed the words.

"You don't leave my side today," he said, leaning close. "Got it?"

"Yeah. Got it."

Oanen narrowed his eyes as if he didn't believe me then started toward the car. When he reached the door, he released me.

"I know you're strong. But I also know you can be hurt. Your safety matters more than Eliana's feelings. More than dead trolls. More than anything else. Do you understand?"

"Yes, Oanen. I get it. I'm glued to you from now until the end of time."

Something flashed in his eyes before he shut them, and he took a slow, deep breath.

"Get in, Megan."

Annoyed and confused, I did as he asked only because arguing would just waste time. He shut the door and walked around toward his side.

"No one likes a bully, Oanen," I said, crossing my arms.

His gaze swung to me through the windshield.

"Stupid bird hearing," I mumbled.

He opened the door, slid behind the wheel, and turned to look at me.

"No," I said, firmly. "No lecture. I'm right next to you,

so there's nothing you need to say except let's go look at a dead troll."

"I think there is something I need to say." He reached out and gently trailed his fingers along my hairline.

"I love you, Megan Smith. And, 'from now until the end of time' is exactly how long I want to be with you."

CHAPTER FIVE

All I could do was stare at Oanen. Love? That was big. I'd known how he felt about me, but I hadn't thought we were to the saying it stage. Saying it was one step closer to white picket fences and babies.

Swallowing hard, I fought the stomach bile rising at the thought of kids. I didn't have my own shit together yet. I couldn't be responsible for someone else. Not for years. And maybe even more years after that.

"Megan, it's getting warm in here," Oanen said. "Why does telling you that I love you make you panic?"

"Can we please not talk about this right now?"

He studied me for a moment.

"You're right. This isn't the place. We'll talk about it tonight."

That did not make me feel any better.

He started the car then carefully pulled into traffic. It took over thirty minutes to reach the warehouse and another ten to find the home of the second troll.

"Who found the body?" I asked, desperate to break the

silence as we walked inside the run-down building. "And why just leave him here? Wasn't there a chance a human could stumble across him?"

"This troll had family who found him. They're with him now."

Oanen knocked and the door immediately opened.

"He's in the bedroom," the troll said, moving aside.

Given my knowledge of trolls, I expected one or two surly relatives. This guy had at least twenty glaring behemoths crammed into a very human-sized apartment.

Oanen took my hand and led the way through the room. I didn't mind his hold this time. My skin crawled with the need to ask the younger troll with the twin black eyes what he'd done.

Only the dead troll waited in the bedroom. He lay on the bed, the mattress bowing under his weight. The smile on his face seemed so out of place after passing through a living room full of scowls.

Oanen released my hand, and I wandered around the room, opening the closet, looking out the window, under the bed.

"I don't know what we're looking for, but I'm pretty sure it's not here," I said, straightening.

Oanen lifted his gaze from his study of the troll.

"You're right," he said.

A shadow filled the doorway behind him a moment before the boy who needed a beating stepped forward. I moved around the bed, but Oanen blocked me. Setting my head against his back, I closed my eyes and listened while trying to ignore my growing anger.

"He knew it was coming," the young troll said.

"Knew what was coming?" Oanen asked.

"His death."

"Why do you think that?"

"I got into some trouble a few weeks back. News spreads fast here. Especially with the old timers. Gramps caught wind and beat me for it. A fair punishment. Better than I'd get from you or the fury I hear is in town. I didn't hate him for it. But, he thought I did. He called me the night before last. Told me he loved me. Shocked me stupid."

"That seems to be a theme today," I mumbled.

Oanen reached back and set his hand on my thigh. Just a simple touch, but it let me know he wasn't mad about my reaction to his declaration.

"Gramps told me to use my head and follow the laws because he wouldn't always be around to watch out for me. Then he hung up. I came by this morning with some goat to let him know we were okay. I found him like this."

"I'm sorry for your loss," Oanen said. "Thank you for sharing what happened with us. You mentioned a fury in town. Any idea where we can find her?"

"No. You know how they work. They can be anywhere."

That made furies sound like the damn boogeyman for supernatural creatures.

Steps shuffled away, and I lifted my head from Oanen's back.

"You all right?" he asked as he faced me.

"Yeah. But, I'll need you to hold my hand on the way out. Whatever that kid did, I want to give him a second beating for it."

No one talked to us as we left, and Oanen didn't release my hand until we reached the car. Anger still poked at me, though. Not from the troll several stories up but from the man walking down the sidewalk.

Oanen's phone chirped as he opened the door for me. I quickly got in and clasped my hands in my lap as Oanen closed the door. The man looked at me through the window, his dark eyes assessing.

Oanen looked up from his phone.

"Keep moving."

I almost grinned at Oanen's possessive tone of voice. Almost. Until I remembered what he'd said last night and just after breakfast.

He waited until the man moved on then went around to his side of the car.

"Please tell me that text had an answer to the smiling troll riddle," I said as he got in.

"No. I had my dad check to see who owned the building you were in last night. The city. Which doesn't help."

"Seriously, Oanen. I don't think whatever was on that burger was meant for me."

"And I don't think it's a coincidence you were dosed with something at the same place that the two trolls, who are now dead, liked to frequent."

"Well, when you put it that way, no, it doesn't sound like a coincidence."

He started the engine and turned around to head back the way we'd come.

"Not to rock the boat, but if getting drugged at the Gizzard is the commonality here, why aren't I dead with a smile on my face?"

His grip on the steering wheel tightened.

"Think about it," I said. "We were there last night, and that troll wasn't."

"We don't know that."

"So we need to go back to the Gizzard and ask."

"Exactly."

We parked a block from the bar and walked the distance in silence. Once again, the atmosphere of downtrodden old people welcomed us when we opened the door. Only this time, the wickedness crawled under my skin as soon as I stepped inside.

With his hand on my back, Oanen steered me toward the bar. The same bartender from the night before came to ask us what we wanted. While I felt anger toward many of the patrons, I didn't feel much for him.

"I want to know what that grey-green powder was on the bacon last night," I said, taking a stool.

"There's no powder on any of the food. Just grease and salt," the man said.

"She ate a bacon cheeseburger here and woke up somewhere else. We need to know what happened," Oanen said.

The bartender studied us for a moment, then the creatures sipping their drinks at the bar, before waving us toward the side door. I glanced at Oanen, and he shrugged and took my hand.

No one paid us much attention as we went to the door. The bartender waited for us just inside the hall coming from the kitchen. Instead of turning that way, the man went to an office to the right.

"I have cameras," he said without preamble. "Five in the main bar, one in the hall, two in the kitchen, and one in this office." He pointed to the monitor on the desk showing nine frames. "The system keeps two months of live feed then purges every ten seconds of video, leaving still frames for six months beyond that. Help yourself."

Oanen sat in the chair and, within a few clicks, had rewound then paused the video to the point where I sat at the bar the night before.

"Has anyone new been coming around?" Oanen asked.

"The odd fellow in the cloak started showing up a few weeks back." The bartender tapped the screen on top of the guy who sat two stools from mine. "Comes every night. Has a drink or two. Talks to whoever's at the bar. Then, he leaves."

"Do you remember if he talked to either of these two trolls?" Oanen asked, pulling up the pictures of the dead, smiling trolls on his phone.

"I serve hundreds of drinks every night. Do you think I remember everyone?"

I had a hard time believing he sold that many drinks, given the meager crowd last night, but I managed to keep my doubt to myself.

Oanen diplomatically did the same and hit the play button. On screen, I watched the dragon turn toward me. Behind him, the cloaked man moved.

"Is there a different angle?" I asked, nudging Oanen.

He pulled up a different window synced at the same timeframe. We all watched the cloaked man reach over, lift the bun, and sprinkle something.

"Right on the damn bacon," I mumbled.

The cloaked man left. The dragon did the same shortly after. I watched the bartender speak with me briefly before I started to eat the burger. Four bites in, I put the burger down and just walked out through the side door.

"I don't remember doing that," I said.

Oanen switched views to the hall outside the office. I went straight out the emergency exit without stopping.

"Did I seriously walk myself to that warehouse?"

"You were gone over three hours," Oanen said. "It's possible. It would explain why you were so cold, too." He turned toward the bartender. "Any idea what he would have put on that burger or where we can find him?"

"I don't know his name, but I can ask around. As for the powder, you might learn more at the Tabernam. I've never heard of anything that trances us."

"Tabernam?" I asked.

"A place where any spell caster can find what they need," Oanen said. He stood and looked at the bartender. "Put the word out that I'm looking for information."

He gave the guy the address of our condo.

THE SMELL OF HERBS, grass, and a hint of smoke filled the air as soon as we opened the door. I inhaled deeply and immediately felt more relaxed.

"I like this place," I said, stepping into the store room filled with aisles of racks. Little bottles and baggies lay in neat rows on each shelf. Some had labels with weird names. Some just said "ask sales associate."

"I'll like this place if we can get some answers," Oanen said.

"You go talk and do your thing, and I'll look for the powder."

"Not a chance. We stick together."

I rolled my eyes and followed him down the center aisle toward the back where a woman stood at a register. She smiled as she watched us with her dark eyes. The curve of her red lips reminded me of a snake. Anger pooled in my stomach. I reached for Oanen's hand to anchor myself. It didn't help much.

He glanced at me and gave my hand a squeeze before turning to the woman.

"Hi. We're looking for a grey-green powder that would put someone in a trance and possibly make them walk somewhere without remembering it."

"I don't sell spells. Only the ingredients to make them."

"What are the ingredients, then?"

She walked around the counter and led the way to the far-left corner. Everything there was labeled with "ask sales associate." A shiver of disquiet raced through me when I saw a bag half filled with deep green powder.

"It's not safe to dabble with things you don't understand," she said, looking at Oanen.

"Do you tell all your customers that?"

"Only the ones who don't look like they have a clue."

"I need a list of names. Everyone who purchased the ingredients needed to work the spell I mentioned."

One side of her mouth lifted in a wry smile.

"I don't ask names. Just for this reason. Anonymity keeps this place in business."

Oanen released my hand and crossed his arms.

"The Council allows a business to continue only through the cooperation of its owner when problems arise."

Her smile faded.

"I don't have any names to give you."

"What do you have?"

The bell above the door chimed. Through the aisles, I caught sight of a cloaked figure walking in.

"Excuse me," the woman said. She quickly headed toward the new arrival.

"Is that the person from the bar?" Oanen asked.

I shook my head. The vibrant red of this cloak couldn't have been further from the dark grey of the cloak from the night before. That, and boobs were filling out the front of it.

"No. It was a man with a dark beard. Not as old as the rest of the crowd in the Gizzard, though."

The saleswoman spoke softly to her new customer and led the woman to another area in the store, closer to us. The lower half of the woman's face felt familiar to me, and I frowned as I strained to hear what they were saying.

"I think I know her," I said softly to Oanen.

"You do?"

"I'm not sure."

I pretended to browse the contents of the racks so I could move closer to the pair. The woman noticed and looked toward us. From behind me, Oanen quietly groaned.

The woman's eyes rounded, and she pushed back her hood.

"Oanen?" she said. She walked to the end of the aisle. Oanen slowly did the same with me now trailing behind. Near the register, they both stopped.

I looked at Oanen, wondering how he knew the woman.

"Hello, Nicolette," he said.

"Darling! It's been too long. How is my baby?"

"Baby?" I said, fighting the strong stirring of jealousy that wanted me to rip her pretty blonde hair from her head.

"She means Eliana," Oanen said, wrapping an arm around me. "Megan, this is Nicolette Barchim, Eliana's mother."

I looked at the woman again, seeing the resemblance. In the hair, nose, and mouth. She didn't look old enough to be Eliana's mom, though. Older sister, maybe.

"Megan?" she said. "Eliana has told me so much about you. I'm happy you arrived in Uttira when you did and relieved you were able to help her make some progress. That girl's issues are enough to make a mother cry, which would destroy my complexion for at least an hour. Tell me how she is. How does she look? Are her curves coming in? Is she feeding enough?"

"I'll go wrap this for you," the saleswoman said, walking behind the counter.

Nicolette's gaze pinged back and forth between Oanen and me as she waited for a response.

"Eliana is well," Oanen said.

"Yeah. She's a good friend."

Nicolette smiled.

"I'm so glad to hear that. I thought that girl would never have a friend. Any lovers yet?"

I glanced at Oanen, unsure what to say. Eliana had told me enough about her mom to know that the woman had completely different methods for childrearing than I'd experienced with my mother.

"No lovers yet," Oanen said. "But as I'm sure Adira has

already reported, she has fed off a grown man and has been wearing more provocative dresses and makeup."

She waved her hand.

"Yes, yes. I know that. I was hoping, living with her, you might have inside information that the starchy Council does not." She stepped closer to Oanen, and he released me, gently nudging me behind him. The protective gesture made me smile.

However, all humor fled the moment she reached out and trailed a finger down his chest.

"If my bedroom were next to yours, there would be no question about whether we were lovers. Off limits always tastes the best."

Jealousy hit me hard right between the eyes and rage quickly followed. I stepped around Oanen and grabbed her wrist.

She yelped, and her eyes turned black.

"You're burning me," she said. "Back off, fledgling."

Oanen moved to stand behind me, our roles reversed. His arms wrapped around my waist, and he nuzzled the back of my head.

"I'm yours," he said softly. "Always."

Nicolette jerked her hand free and stared at me with her wide, black eyes. I let my anger show in mine, and her face lit with a soft orange glow.

"Don't ever touch him again," I said, my voice carrying a hint of the fury echo.

"This is interesting," she said, her cheeks flushing from the heat I knew I was putting off. "A griffin and a fury. Tell me, dear. Does your mother know?"

It pissed me off that she wasn't even showing a hint of fear or concern.

"I doubt it. My mom has been out of the picture since she left me in Uttira."

Nicolette tsked.

"It's a shame when our kind abandons their young. I would have never done that to Eliana if she hadn't fought so hard to be allowed to develop her skills on her own."

"Go, Nicolette," Oanen said from behind me. "Now."

Nicolette set some money on the counter, without looking away from us, and accepted her wrapped package from the shopkeeper.

"I'm sure I'll see you around, Fury," she said with a nod of her head. "Delicious to see you again, Oanen. Maybe next time I'll get a taste."

His arms tightened around me, keeping me from flying at her.

Her sultry laugh followed her out the door. I turned my angry gaze on the saleswoman. I could feel her nervousness and a hint of something wicked that wasn't there a few moments ago.

"Do all your customers wear cloaks?" I asked.

"Only the ones who want to keep their identities secret," she said.

I pulled Oanen's arms free of my waist and stepped up to the counter. The woman cringed when I leaned toward her.

"No more secrets. Start taking names or you'll be confessing whatever it is I'm sensing. Do you understand?"

"Yes, Fury."

Oanen said nothing as I turned and stormed out of the

shop. The cool winter air caressed my cheeks as I stood on the sidewalk with my eyes closed for a few minutes.

"You okay?" he asked.

"Yeah. Eliana's mother is—"

"A succubus," he said. "And Eliana will be grateful you didn't hurt her."

I opened my eyes and looked at him.

"Are you sure about that?"

He shrugged and laced his fingers through mine, a hint of humor making his lips twitch.

"You hungry?"

"I could eat."

Forty minutes later, we were seated in a diner whose patrons made my skin crawl. Nothing overwhelming, individually, just a whole lot of messed up, collectively. Based on the tingle that had raced over my skin walking through the door of the café, I knew it was another Mantirum-only establishment, which explained the overall whisper of wickedness. Eating somewhere else might have been more pleasant, but at least here we could talk freely.

"How are we supposed to find out what's happening when no one seems to know anything?" I asked, opening a menu.

Oanen wasn't the least bit put off by my surly attitude.

"We'll find something soon. Word will spread that we're looking for information. Between the bar and Tabernam, someone will have something for us.

A waitress stopped at our table and set two glasses of water down.

"Griffins never could see what was right in front of their faces," she said. "The victims were all males and all trolls.

What do you think would leave a troll with a smile on his face? And, I hear there's a pregnant one in the city. You know what that means."

She winked at me. Clueless, I looked at Oanen for an explanation as the waitress moved off.

"She's talking about a succubus," he said.

"You don't think—"

"Eliana's mom is responsible? I don't know, but we need to find out."

# CHAPTER SIX

OANEN STOOD AND HELD OUT HIS HAND TO ME. I MADE A face, tossed down the menu, and joined him.

"I thought I'd be eating like a pig in New York. Instead, I'm going to starve," I grumbled.

He gave my hand a gentle squeeze and led me out to the street. On the sidewalk, he turned toward me and cupped my face.

"After this, it'll be just you, me, and an extra-large pizza."

"Don't toy with me, bird boy. You better deliver."

He tilted his head and studied my face for a moment.

"Are you okay?" he asked.

"I'm hungry, and we're leaving the place that could have fixed that. What do you think?"

"I think it's not food that's upsetting you. Your eyes have just a hint of orange to them."

His words brought my attention to the wickedness slowly coating my skin. I opened myself to the source.

"Who is it?" Oanen said softly.

The wickedness came from everywhere. From everyone to one degree or another.

"Crap," I said under my breath. "I just can't catch a break." I grabbed Oanen's hand again and hustled toward the car.

"What's going on?" he asked.

"Let's just hurry before I go after someone here on the street."

"It's more than one person?" he asked, opening my door.

"It's everyone."

He frowned at me as I got in but didn't say anything more.

The need to jump out of the car grew stronger on the drive to the Tabernam, and I didn't understand why. Well, I did. But given how I'd been fine the day before, I didn't understand why people on the street and in passing cars were suddenly adding to the anger coating me with each passing second.

"I think I should take you home," he said when we were only a block away.

"Why? We're almost there."

His hand covered my fist. I made a face and tried to relax my fingers. It wasn't easy. The need to do something, to punish someone, rode me hard.

"I'll be fine."

However, once inside the Tabernam, my mind went back to how Eliana's mom had hit on Oanen, and my anger only grew. Had the succubus still been there, I would have owed Eliana a sympathy card.

Oanen stopped my forward progress with an arm

around my waist. Before I could tell him to let go, he turned me, grabbed my head and planted a kiss on me that made me forget the anger threading its way under my skin.

When he pulled back, the orange glow from my eyes reflected off his face. Only this time, it wasn't anger.

"You are the most beautiful creature in this world," he said softly. "And, it's hard to think straight when your eyes glow like that."

"Then maybe you should stop randomly kissing me," I said.

"Never."

I rolled my eyes at him, and his lips quirked at the corners.

"We're here for a reason," I reminded him.

"Hopefully it's to purchase something." The familiar voice killed the happy glow Oanen's lips had created.

Clenching my fists, I turned toward the clerk.

"Creatures are dying. I'm skipping meals to chase down answers. And, I'm fighting the urge to throat punch someone. Do you seriously think we're here to buy something?"

"Nicolette Barchim, the succubus," Oanen said, setting his hands on my shoulders. "What did she buy?"

I could see the hesitation in the woman's eyes.

"Do not make me pull out my Fury," I warned.

The woman blanched and quickly answered.

"Herbs."

"Not good enough. What herbs? What are they for?"

"They're harmless. Just a boost to her energy while she's pregnant."

"Thank you," Oanen said.

The next thing I knew, I was in his arms and on the way out of the shop.

"I can walk," I said scowling up at him.

"And, I can carry you. It was my turn."

"You're ridiculous."

"No. I'm in a hurry. I promised you pizza, and you were looking ready for a fight."

He set me down on the sidewalk and opened the car door for me.

"I'm sorry I didn't feed you first."

"You better be."

I got in and buckled up. On the drive back, he asked me to message what we'd learned to his dad.

"Don't you think you should let Eliana know first? I mean, it is her mom."

"And if it's her mom killing creatures because she's trying to feed Eliana's new sibling?"

Eliana already hated what she was. I couldn't imagine how much it would freak her out if she learned her mom was killing creatures because she was pregnant.

"Point taken. I didn't think their kind killed to feed." Although, I did remember Eliana's concern that she'd killed the guy in the alley.

"A succubus typically feeds off of sexual energy, not life energy. They can weaken their meal to the point of unconsciousness. Once unconscious, there's no sexual energy."

"These killings don't sound like a succubus, then?"

"They don't sound like anything we know."

I typed out a brief message—*Eliana's mom is preggers*—and hit send.

"Now, about this pizza."

"Anything you want," he said. "It's New York. Just about everywhere delivers."

"Pizza. Pepperoni is a must. Along with bacon, green olives, and onion."

He glanced at me.

"That's an unusual combination."

"Am I a usual person?"

We talked about other food quirks on the way to his parents' place. I tried to play it cool like his talk was distracting me but knew I'd failed when he covered my fist with his hand again. The anger, along with a familiar restlessness, was still building. If I were back home, I would go for a run. That wasn't an option here, though.

As soon as he parked, I opened my door and hurried for the entrance.

His hand smoothed down my back the moment we were inside.

"It'll be better in the condo. It's protected."

I hoped he was right. Using the stairs as an outlet, I sprinted upward, taking the steps two at a time.

"There's a treadmill in the living room closet," Oanen said as he reached around me to open the door. I liked that he always kept up with me.

"A treadmill in the closet?"

I looked at the double doors on the opposite wall.

"You're not the only person to get restless."

He closed the door then crossed the room to pull out the treadmill. As soon as he had the track down, he started it and motioned me forward.

"I'll order the pizza while you run."

"Thank you."

I cranked the speed up, testing myself and the machine as I went all out. I wasn't winded by the time I finished but managed to work up a bit of a sweat and purge some of the restlessness.

"Better?" Oanen asked when I shut the machine off.

"Much. How long until the pizza gets here?"

"Another fifteen minutes."

"Perfect."

I took a quick shower and put on last night's pajamas. Since there was still time before dinner arrived, I used it to call Eliana. She answered on the first ring.

"Any sign of the brownie or goblin yet?" I asked.

"Not yet." She didn't sound like herself.

"What's wrong?"

"Nothing."

"Are you trying to lie to me?"

"Yes. Because I want you to focus on getting the job done so you can get home sooner."

"Talk, succubus."

Eliana sighed.

"I didn't know how lonely I was until I made a friend and she left. And then, I find out someone is trying to kill her and my only friend might not come back."

"I miss you, too. And that burger wasn't meant for me. Oanen overreacted because of the whole bird bond thing. As for the smiling dead trolls, we have a few leads. It shouldn't be too much longer. I'm coming back. I promise. How did it go at the academy today?"

"Good. Eugene is loving classes and asking a ton of questions. It rubbed a few people wrong, but by the end of the day, I think they were catching on that Eugene is impressed and curious and not a threat. Oh, a siren almost got him into the pool at lunch, but Ashlyn was there to block him. And, Fenris was being pretty good about keeping an eye on the humans, too."

"Oh? So you and Fenris were hanging out?"

She snorted.

"No way. He keeps texting me annoying updates. I think he misses you."

"Then, I think you should be a friend and keep him company."

"Not me," she said, sounding completely panicked. "I think the new girls are stirring his wolfie hormones or something because he's getting worse."

"Worse? You mean he's flirting?"

"No. He hasn't changed at all in that way. It's his lust. I can barely be in the same room with him. When I spot him now, I just go the other way."

I felt bad for Fenris and wondered what kind of miracle it was going to take for Eliana to figure out that all Fenris' lust had everything to do with her. I could only imagine how desperate he was starting to feel if Eliana thought his lust was worse than before.

"How's your succubus training going? Adira still dressing you?"

"She set out clothes for me this morning. I got creative with them while still following the rules. I wish everyone around here would just leave me alone. I might be a little on the small side, but I don't think I'm unhealthy. Nothing to warrant this much unwanted attention."

In the living room, the doorbell rang. I opened the door and waved to Oanen as he left to get the pizza.

"So how is it staying in New York? Are you missing your backpack with all the wicked you're running into? Did you kill anyone yet?" Eliana asked.

"Not yet. It's weird here. Most of the time, it's not as provoking as I thought it would be. People I would have thought I'd want to beat the hell out of, like Elbner, don't bug me. Yet today, regular people were starting to get under my skin. I'm just glad it's not like it was the night I came here with Adira. That would have been hell. As it is, I think New York would be more fun if we weren't having to deal with dying trolls."

"I heard Adira and the Quills talking. While you're checking out the deaths in New York, the council near Flagstaff is investigating the deaths of three Nemean lions."

"What's a Nemean lion and did they die with smiles, too?" She laughed.

"No. Nemean lions are a lot like regular lions. They're animals but a lot harder to kill. Their coats are impenetrable by mortal blades. Since they're a protected species by our laws, the word is going out, asking for information about their deaths."

"I'm not sure how this is supposed to make me feel better about dealing with troll deaths."

"It's not. I told you so you'd know the Council isn't giving Oanen all the poopy jobs. An enforcer has to look into any death that's questionable."

"Poopy?" I said with a laugh. "Adira should forget the succubus clothes and work on your language skills."

"Swearing isn't a language skill."

"Says the person who doesn't know how."

"I know how, I just choose not to."

I snorted at her as the door opened and Oanen strode in carrying the pizza. The smell of it hit me hard and made my stomach growl.

"I better go. Oanen just walked in with our pizza, and I'm starving."

"Tell him I said hi. Talk to you tomorrow."

I hung up and hurried to the pizza. Oanen's lips twitched as I hungrily watched him open the box.

"That smells amazing," I said, inhaling.

"I'll let you have some if you sit on the couch and watch a movie with me."

"You had me at 'I'll let you have some.'"

He chuckled and set a huge slice on a plate for me. The tip of the wedge hung off the edge. I sat on the couch and dug in while he started the movie.

I ate three slices the size of my head before I pushed my plate away with a groan.

"Best pizza ever."

"Feel better?" he asked.

"I do. Thank you."

He wrapped an arm around my shoulders, pulled me close, and pressed his lips against the top of my temple. I leaned into his side and exhaled contentedly, only partially focused on the movie. My mind continued to dwell on the troll deaths and Eliana's mom. It would devastate Eliana if her mom was responsible for them. Eliana already hated what she was and feared what she'd become.

That kind of fear was something with which I could

empathize. As much as I'd pushed aside what I learned in the *Book of Fury*, I dreaded what gaining my full powers would mean for me. Without a doubt, Eliana and I were in the same boat, and I couldn't help but wonder what the future would hold for both of us.

Oanen's hand smoothed over my arm.

"That was a big sigh for an action movie," he said.

"Sorry. I didn't realize I sighed. I was just thinking about the future."

He paused the movie.

"You didn't need to do that. I'll stop talking."

"I paused it so you would keep talking. The future…our future…is something that very much interests me."

The low rumble of his voice and the way the flecks of gold in his blue eyes multiplied as I watched sent up warning flags. Our conversation from earlier, or rather, what he'd declared earlier, came back to me in a rush. He loved me and wanted forever.

I swallowed hard, wondering what I should say. I didn't want to talk relationship. Not now. Not this close to bedtime.

"What are you thinking that's making you blush?" he asked.

He leaned in slowly, and my pulse picked up speed. His lips quirked at the corners just before his mouth touched mine. The taste of him set off a storm, and fire and lightning exploded inside of me.

My head spun, and I gripped the front of his shirt tightly, anchoring myself and holding him in place. He leaned in further, causing me to slowly slide down into the cushions. The weight of him warmed me. The feel of his chest against mine made it hard to breathe as want consumed me. I wanted to feel all of him pressed against all of me. My body ached for that much contact.

I tore my mouth from his, struggling to remember why we needed to stop. Why I couldn't wrap a leg around his waist and pull him closer.

It wasn't easy to think clearly when his mouth was trailing kisses down my throat. Images of us tangled in sheets, his hands sliding over my bare skin, filled my mind and left me breathless.

I wanted him so much it hurt. My fingers itched to inch their way up his shirt. To remove his clothing. To make the images in my mind a reality.

The stroke of his tongue against the edge of my ear sent me flying off the couch. With that touch, the reason we shouldn't pushed its way forward.

He chuckled, his golden eyes pinning me.

"Not your thing?"

I stared at him for a moment, debating what to say. He caught my hesitation and grew serious.

"Talk to me," he said softly.

I let out a slow breath.

"When we kiss like that, it's hard to remember why I need to say no."

"Why do you need to say no?"

"We're eighteen. I don't want to start a family at eighteen. I'm not even sure I'll want to start a family at fifty. I mean, I'm barely holding my own shit together. There's no way I want the responsibility of caring for someone else."

He watched me for a moment, really considering my words.

"Sex doesn't need to mean kids. I'm not saying that to try to talk you into something you're not ready for. I'm saying it to let you know I'm okay with waiting for kids."

He stood and closed the distance between us.

"And, I'm okay waiting for you."

Even though he said the thing that should have soothed me, I was stuck on one word.

"Kids? Plural? Shoot me now."

He chuckled and pulled me close, kissing me gently.

"Baby griffins are adorable," he said, holding me. "Picture a chicken-sized griffin."

I groaned.

"I'm never going to look at you the same way, again," I said.

"What? You said you liked my beak."

"You should stop now."

"I'm hoping if I keep talking, you'll get desperate enough to kiss me like we both want."

"Remember you asked for this, bird boy," I said a moment before I lifted my head and claimed his lips. It was his turn to groan. He clutched me close as my tongue teased his. As my hands slipped under his shirt. As I stood on my toes and pressed my hips against his.

A moment later, he had me in his arms and was walking toward the bedroom.

"Wait," I said, breaking the kiss.

"Now who's the chicken?" he said. "We're just going to bed."

"While kissing. I'm not stupid."

"No sex tonight, Megan. I want to feel your lips against mine until we both pass out. I want it to be the last thing I remember before closing my eyes, and the first thing I think of when I open them again. I know you're not ready for more; just like I know you'll let me know when you are ready."

I looked up at him, tangling my fingers in his hair.

"Just a hella lot of kissing then?" I asked.

"And maybe some petting. I hear birds like that."

I grinned at his deadpan delivery.

"I think I can handle that," I said before kissing him again.

ANGER FLOODED me with a suffocating fullness. I woke, breathing slowly and deeply. The smell of warm cotton tickled my nose, and I carefully slid from Oanen's arms, our heavy make out session barely a thought.

An invisible line pulled me from the bedroom. Barefoot, I padded across the living room toward the sunroom and balcony. Someone very wicked moved out there.

I smiled in anticipation and opened the door.

"Come to confess?" I asked the creature that straightened from the shadows.

His humorless black eyes found mine as I closed the distance between us. He reeked of blood, booze, and fear. I inhaled deeply and didn't stop walking until we stood toe to toe with his back against the metal and glass rail.

Even though I could smell his fear, it didn't reflect in his gaze or his words.

"Not in this life, little girl. You need to leave town. Now."

Lightning fast, I grabbed his throat and lifted him high.

"I'm not the one leaving town. You are. Hell's waiting for you."

"Hell's for humans, bitch," he rasped.

"We'll see about that. Elwood Rumlar, confess." The word brought him to his knees like all the others. He shook, and anger filled his gaze as he spoke of his crimes. He'd killed. Eaten human flesh. Broken the laws of humans and non-humans, alike.

The rage inside of me roared to life and fire danced up my arm.

"Elwood Rumlar, you've earned your place in hell."

I embraced my fury power as I reached for his throat. Before I touched him, pain exploded inside of me from head to toe like I was being ripped in two.

I opened my mouth to scream, but no sound emerged as blackness consumed me.

MY PULSE THUMPED in my head. Opening my eyes, I blearily stared at the snow-dusted surface before me. The patio floor. I'd fallen. Again.

I tried to sit up and hissed at the pain searing my chest. I looked down at another burn mark.

"Fuck."

Oanen was going to notice this one.

Getting to my feet, I looked for the thing that had drawn me outside. I was alone. However the creature had gotten out there, it seemed it had left the same way.

Pre-dawn light reflected off the sunroom glass. I looked

over my shoulder in surprise. How much time had passed since I'd gone outside? Obviously half the night. Suppressing a shiver, I used my cold, stiff fingers to open the door.

I went straight for the shower. Oanen would definitely notice how cold I was if I tried crawling into bed with him. The hot water felt good on everything but the burn. I gritted my teeth through washing and drying and put the same cream on the new burn as Oanen had put on the old one. When I finished, I wrapped the towel around my torso and crept out of the bathroom to grab myself some clean clothes. Escaping to the living room to dress, I noted the sun was just clearing the horizon.

"So much for going back to bed," I muttered to myself.

Despite having been passed out for hours, I was exhausted. I pulled on my clothes, careful of the new injury. Dressed and slowly toweling my hair, I stared out at the patio.

Other than wicked and not human, I didn't know what that thing had been or why it had come here in the first place.

I thought back to everything he'd said. He'd wanted me to leave town. Why? Was he trying to warn me away from the troll deaths? Were we getting close to finding the killer?

"You're up early," Oanen said from behind me, causing me to startle.

I looked back at him. He wore a pair of shorts, leaving his gloriously golden chest bare for my enjoyment. If only my head wasn't pounding.

"You're up early, too."

"It's not as fun sleeping late without you beside me. Your spot was cold. How long have you been up?"

"Not long," I said. It was the truth, but not what he meant.

I tossed my towel onto the couch and walked toward him, knowing I needed to distract him from his current line of questioning. There was no way I was going to admit I passed out on the patio for the past several hours.

"I thought the first thing you wanted to think about in the morning was a kiss."

His lips curved in a sexy half-smile, and he met me in the middle of the room.

"You would be correct." He wrapped his arms around me and pulled me close.

I almost winced at the sting from the heat of his chest on my burn.

"Do I detect a hint of minty freshness?" I asked instead.

"I heard you in the shower," he said.

"And you missed your chance to join me?"

Gold pooled in Oanen's eyes.

"Don't tease me, Fury."

CHAPTER SEVEN

GRINNING, I STOOD ON MY TOES TO KISS OANEN LIGHTLY AND pulled back before he could take things further.

"We're in food-central, and I'm starving. Something just isn't right about this."

He sighed and brushed his fingers along my jaw.

"I know you're nervous," he said.

My pulse jumped, and I reached up to the neckline of my shirt. There was no way he could see it, could he?

"I meant what I said. I'll wait for as long as it takes. Just don't stop kissing me."

Relief coursed through me. He'd meant sex, not the burns. I found it ironic that I found sex a safe topic this morning.

"If you want more kisses, feed me."

My stomach let out a growl.

He grinned, kissed my forehead, then left me so he could shower.

Less than twenty minutes later, we were seated in a familiar diner.

"Is one of everything an option?" I asked, studying the choices and seeing too many things I'd want to try if my head didn't hurt so much.

"Are you sure you're feeling okay?"

"Hey, no judging a girl with a healthy appetite."

"Not that. You can get whatever you want. You just look a little pale today."

"I'm fine, Oanen." But, I was starting to think I wasn't. This was twice now that I'd been burned trying to use my powers. Once in the parking lot and now on the patio. Both times I tried to send someone to hell. Obviously, I was doing something wrong. But, the *Book of Fury* didn't exactly outline the steps to a successful trip to hell.

After the waitress took our order, he reached across the table and played with my fingers.

"I know we're not supposed to talk about this, but you're different. I think something's wrong."

I opened my mouth to say I was fine again, but he lifted his hand.

"Hear me out. Before the lake, you ran hot. Now, you get cold. You threw up. You're not sensing the wicked like you used to. And you have a burn that's not healing as quickly as it should. I'm worried."

His phone rang, but he didn't move to answer it.

"Adira, Mom, and Dad are worried too."

"You told them?"

He took his phone out of his pocket and met my gaze.

"There isn't anything I wouldn't do for you. Including risk your temper to keep you safe. I'll be right back."

He stood and strode toward the exit while my mouth was still hanging open. He would flip his shit if he found out I had another burn. My gaze tracked him as he walked outside and stood on the sidewalk to answer his phone.

Across from me, someone sat in his place.

I turned, and my jaw almost dropped for a second time.

"You're wasting time," Mom said.

She looked exactly the same. I struggled between wanting to hug her and wanting to punch her in the face because of ditching me. I surprised us both by partially standing and hugging her. She set her cheek against my head and stroked a hand down my hair. Too quickly, she pulled away.

"You need to get to your Grandma Irene."

"Why?" I asked, trying not to let my frustration show.

"I told you. You can't deliver the wicked to hell without your wings because without them, you're not a fury, and your power will consume you."

The straight forward answer stunned me. She took advantage of my silence to continue.

"Ditch the unnecessary baggage and get to St. Louis."

"Baggage?" I asked, confused.

Mom's gaze flicked to Oanen, who had his back to us.

"Oanen isn't baggage. He's my boyfriend."

A wave of heat came from across the table.

"Have you slept with him?" she demanded.

"We're staying at his parents' apartment. There's only one bed."

"Stop being thick. Have you had sex?"

I didn't like her tone or the anger in her expression.

"You ditched me, remember? I think that means my sex life is none of your business."

"Of course it is. Didn't you learn anything in that shit

town? Griffins only have sons. Furies only have daughters. It will never work. You will destroy each other."

"It's a little late for that warning. We're already bonded."

Her expression changed, becoming more earnest.

"Learn from your succubus friend. The boy can love you, but you don't need to love him."

There was so much wrong in what she just said. How did she know about Eliana? And was her attitude the reason for the revolving door of her love life?

"You should have listened to the messenger. It's dangerous for us to keep meeting. I'm guessing you already have your first burn or you wouldn't be this calm."

"Hold up," I said. "Messenger? You mean you sent that guy last night?"

She exhaled slowly, a look of annoyance crossing her features before she suppressed it.

"You need to focus, Megan. Your power is free, uncontrolled and unpredictable, and it will burn you out if you don't get your ass to your great-grandma's place in St. Louis and kill her so you can claim your power as a fury in full. Do you understand? I didn't bring you into this world just to watch you die before your time."

A waitress walked over with my chocolate milk.

"Get it done," Mom said, sliding out of her seat.

"Wait."

She left without a backward glance. As much as I wanted to push the waitress out of the way and chase her down, I stayed in my seat.

"Your food will be out in a minute," the waitress said before walking away again.

I barely heard her. The gas station. The man on the balcony. If Mom was being honest, things were worse than I'd thought. And, they'd keep going downhill from here.

Heart sinking, I glanced out the window at Oanen. I couldn't tell him what Mom had said. He'd made the priority of my well-being pretty plain. And I couldn't—no, I wouldn't—kill my great-grandma just to save myself. There had to be another way. If it was my power burning me up because I was trying to send people to hell, then I'd stop trying to send them. How hard could it be?

Oanen pocketed his phone and headed for the door. I took a drink of chocolate milk and focused on trying to calm down. By the time he strode in, I was able to arch a brow at him.

"And what was so important that you needed to run away before I could unleash my anger?"

His lips twitched a little as he sat down.

"Your anger has never concerned me."

"Oh, you're begging for it now."

"I thought I've been begging for it since the moment we met," he said.

I frowned at the gold creeping into his gaze.

"We're not talking about the same thing anymore, are we?"

A small grin tugged at his lips before disappearing. He was breathtaking when mischievous and amused.

"That was Adira," he said, answering my original question.

The waitress interrupted with the delivery of our food. I dug into my pancakes and waited for Oanen to continue.

"The Council believes that Eliana's mom is tied to the murders."

"Why?"

"All the victims are males. The smiles in death. And the fact that pregnant succubi are ravenous enough to easily be one of the most dangerous creatures out there. The Council wants us to investigate Nicolette further."

I sighed and took another big, syrup and butter-soaked bite.

"So are you going to tell me what your mom wanted?" Oanen said.

My heart gave a hard thump as I swallowed.

"You saw?"

"After you disappeared from the Gizzard, I'll never fully take my eyes off you again."

I took a sip of my milk while I tried to think what to say. I didn't want to lie. He'd know if I did. Omission wasn't far from lying, either. But I told myself I wasn't going to hide what I knew forever. Just until I could figure out a way for me to live without someone else dying.

"She pulled her normal Paxton bullshit," I said finally. "She wanted to know if we've had sex. When I told her it was none of her business, she said that griffins only have male offspring and furies female. That we can't mix. She wants me to get rid of you."

Oanen's eyes darkened.

"There is no going back," he said. "We're bonded."

"I told her that. It didn't matter to her. It seems like babies are on everyone's brains."

He exhaled slowly.

"I'm not sure how much we can trust what she says.

Like the Council, your mother seems to be withholding information."

"Exactly. The information that she gives is reliable enough, but there are too many holes and missing bits for us to clearly see the big picture."

"Maybe we should go to your great-grandmother."

My heart stopped before my anger started to surge. He held up a hand.

"Not to do what your mom wants but to ask questions. Maybe your Grandma Irene would be more willing to share some straight forward answers."

I considered what he was suggesting.

"Okay. We can try talking to her. Hopefully she's more mellow than Paxton."

We finished our meal and, with renewed determination, left the diner. Oanen wanted to re-check the places the trolls had died for any clues that might point to Nicolette.

In the kitchen space of the first apartment we went to, the ceiling was slowly giving up its hold and crumbling down to the floor in hand-sized chunks. Some of those chunks had been crushed to small mounds of dust that intermingled with other debris. Old food wrappers. Small bones. Shredded bits of material. Thankfully, the heat was off so the place didn't smell too bad.

"What type of clues are we looking for?" I asked as I studied the place.

"I'm not sure," Oanen admitted.

"If Nicolette is anything like Eliana, I can't see her setting foot in here, no matter how hungry she is. I mean, Eliana's too…clean."

He looked around the efficiency apartment, his eyes

lingering on the tattered bare mattress, dark with who knew what kinds of stains, and shook his head.

"You're right. I don't see any succubus willingly coming in here."

"If I remember right, the other apartment was better than this one, and that one still was something I couldn't picture Nicolette willingly visiting. When we saw her in the Tabernam, she wore a nice cloak and her nails were a perfectly polished red that matched her lipstick. My point is that she was put together. High class, not streetwalker, put together."

"Maybe she didn't go home with them. Maybe they went to her home."

"And she carried them back to their places after feeding?" I asked. "It doesn't fit her upscale you're-beneath-me vibe. The way she acts, she expects guys to carry her, not the other way around."

"You were in Uttira for several months. We're taught to blend. To not leave a trail. It's possible she could have left her kill in a location where no one would suspect her. I think the proof we need won't be here but at the Goose and Gizzard on those tapes."

"Alright. Let's go." Although I didn't like the idea of going back there again, I was willing to do just about anything to get out of this apartment.

Oanen led the way and opened the car door for me. Across the street, a group of young men openly watched us with looks of hostility on their faces. Not a hint of wickedness touched me. Mom's words came back to me. *I'm guessing you already have your first burn or you wouldn't be this calm.*

"You're not feeling anything from them, are you?" Oanen asked, noting my hesitation.

"No. Nothing." I looked up at him and gave him a quick kiss. "Stay focused on the case," I said. "I'll be fine."

He didn't say anything as I got in, and he closed the door. But he was right. I should have been able to sense something from them. Their body language alone said they were up to no good.

When he pulled away from the curb, he didn't turn around and head back to the Gizzard.

"Aren't we going the wrong way?"

"Nope. The Gizzard won't be open for a while, and I promised to keep you fed."

"But we just had breakfast."

"We're going somewhere for fun then food."

He took 278 south to Ocean Parkway. I paid attention to the tree lined boulevard, feeling a sense of familiarity that I couldn't quite place. It'd been a long time since I'd been in New York. When we turned onto Surf Avenue, and I saw the red spire on the horizon, I knew where we were going.

"Coney Island?"

"Have you been there already?" he asked.

"Yeah, but a long time ago. I remember it was great, though."

The remnants of my headache faded as I leaned forward in my seat and waited for the first glimpse of the rollercoaster. My memories of the amusement park were of people, good food, games, and rides. So, it happened a long time before I started losing my temper. I frowned slightly and hoped I wouldn't ruin it this time, either.

Oanen found a place to park, and hand in hand, we

strolled down the boardwalk. The sights, sounds, and smells filled me with excitement.

"What do you want to do first?" he asked.

"All of it."

We moved from ride to ride. He grinned at my enthusiasm and shook his head when I suggested the roller coaster be renamed to Soaring Griffin.

"It's pretty close to flying with you," I said.

"I doubt that."

"You weren't the one clinging to your back when you dove down at Aubrey in that clearing."

After we'd had enough of the rides, he humored me with a few games. Most of them would have been hard for a human to win. I delighted in making the booth attendees' jaws drop when I bested them.

"I think your stuffed animal collection is big enough," Oanen said, his voice muffled by a unicorn's fluffy pink tail.

I picked the animal off the pile and handed it to the nearest kid.

"Let's find some new owners for the rest of these then get something to eat," I said.

The toys were easy to get rid of. Deciding where to eat was harder. We settled on hot dogs and went to sit shoulder to shoulder on the beach, listening to the waves as we ate.

It felt like a date. Not the secluded, come-to-my-house-and-have-a-quiet-dinner kind but a real date.

"Thank you for this," I said when we'd finished eating. "It felt so...normal."

"The first date of many that will be like this," he said, his gaze sweeping over my features in a way that made my pulse skip. When he leaned toward me, I met him eagerly.

His lips touched mine, and his arms wrapped around me, careful to avoid the burn on my back. I barely had time to note that before he deepened the kiss and stole my ability to reason or breathe. Oanen was my world. Then and always.

When he pulled back and broke the kiss moments later, the cool ocean breeze brought clarity as I tried to catch my breath.

I liked kissing Oanen. Talking to him. Sleeping beside him. Just being with him. No, it wasn't like. It was so much more than like. And, that still scared the hell out of me.

He watched me closely, his golden gaze missing nothing.

"I love the fire in your eyes and the way you look at me after we kiss. I see every bit of passion your fear is holding back, and it makes my heart race because, I know when you unleash it, not even the gods will be able to keep us apart."

"Oanen, I…"

His lips twitched as he watched me fumble with what to say.

"I know the time's not right for you to admit how much you can't live without me. Don't worry; I'm patient."

His teasing helped with the awkwardness.

"Patient? I would have gone with overconfident. Now, don't we have some tapes to look at?" I said, standing and brushing my butt off.

He chuckled and joined me.

"Here, let me help."

I hopped away before he could touch me.

"Hands to yourself. You've messed with my head enough for one day."

He studied my face for a long moment.

"I've meant everything I've said. Kids don't matter. Sex doesn't matter. You admitting how you feel about me doesn't matter. You're all that matters."

He was getting into the scary territory again. I thought of my burns and my great-grandma and needed to shift the topic.

"That's not what I meant. I meant all this talk about kissing and passion is distracting me from our focus."

"That is my focus, Megan. You."

"Dead trolls, Oanen. That's our focus. And Nicolette. Come on."

There was no handholding on the way back to the car. I was too rattled and worried. I loved Oanen loving me. Although the idea of kids still scared the hell out of me, I trusted him when he said having kids wasn't something we needed to do right away. I also trusted that he would wait and let me drive the pace of our physical and emotional relationship. It was his complete need to keep me safe that worried me. What would he do when he found out about the second burn? Or that these burns were signs of my powers eating me alive?

The car ride to the Gizzard was just as quiet.

As soon as we walked into the place, we had the bartender's attention. He nodded to the side door and moved to meet us in the short hall.

"No news, Enforcer. Words out, but no one's talking."

"I was wondering if we could look at your tapes for the past several weeks."

"Knock yourself out. Want me to bring you anything to eat or drink?"

"No, thank you," Oanen and I said at the same time.

The man left us alone in the back room for the next two hours. Oanen and I watched endless footage of patrons coming and going. Eating and drinking. We didn't see much conversation happening. And, there definitely were no signs of a put together succubus.

"There's nothing here to link Nicolette to the troll deaths. I'm going to call Eliana."

Oanen grabbed my hand before I could pull my phone free.

"You can't call her," he said.

I narrowed my eyes at him.

"She's my best friend, who I promised to call every day. If I don't call her, she'll be angry."

He removed his hand.

"Don't say anything about her mom."

"You've already said that."

I dialed Eliana. Like the last time, she picked up on the first ring.

"Where's the seventies porn background music?" I asked.

"What? Ew! Why would you say that?"

I laughed.

"I figured Adira would have converted you by now."

She snorted.

"No. She's been surprisingly quiet today."

And I knew why.

"So, I have some interesting news," I said.

Oanen turned in his chair and crossed his arms at me. I rolled my eyes at him.

"I saw my mom today," I said to Eliana.

"No way. Did she tell you what's going on?"

"Yep. Apparently Oanen and I can't be together because griffins have boy baby chickens and furies have girls with anger issues. According to her, we won't mix."

"While she might be right about the past, who's to say what will happen? I don't think a griffin and fury pairing has ever been done before. At least not in written history."

"I just wish she didn't try so hard to be a pain in my ass, you know?"

"I'm sorry it wasn't a pleasant reunion."

"It wasn't as bad as it could have been, I guess. She looked exactly the same. But, this time when I saw her, I realized just how much I didn't know about her. Other than her taste in men. But back then, I thought she was just a regular, human gold digger, you know?"

"My mom's motto is usually the richer, the better."

I gave Oanen a triumphant look.

"Usually?"

"Apparently my dad was an exception." A morose note crept into Eliana's voice. "His devotion tasted sweeter because it had never been given to a mortal before. Only to one of the gods."

"Hey. I didn't mean to bring you down. Let's talk about something else. Anything interesting happen at the Academy today?"

"Not really. I better go. It's just about dinner time, and if I get down there first, I can be sitting before Adira arrives."

"Um?"

"She won't notice my dress enough to make me change."

"Ah. Okay. I'll talk to you tomorrow."

After I hung up, I gave Oanen a pointed look.

"And that confirms it. Nicolette would never go to a dive like this to pick up men. She'd go upscale."

The monitor behind Oanen caught my attention.

"Look," I said, pointing at the screen. "There he is again."

"It's the same cloak," Oanen agreed. He changed the angle to find a camera with a shot of the guy's face, but it was never a clear look.

"It's like he knows where the cameras are."

Oanen made a sound of agreement then froze the frame.

"That's him. The troll grandpa who beat his grandson."

He was sitting right next to the cloaked man.

"I need to call the Council. But not from here," he said, standing. "Let's pick up something to eat and head back to our place."

## CHAPTER EIGHT

WARM WATER GENTLY TAPPED AGAINST MY BACK. THE SORE there had healed enough for a shower without pain. However, the sore on my front was another story. It still looked raw and red.

Thankfully, Oanen hadn't commented when I'd stolen one of his t-shirts to sleep in last night instead of my usual tank top. I smiled at the memory of how his eyes had heated when he'd seen me in his clothes. Nope, he hadn't minded a bit.

I finished rinsing my hair and turned off the water. Just as I stepped out of the shower, the bathroom door started to open. I grabbed the towel and managed to cover my chest before Oanen saw anything.

His heated gaze swept over me from head to toe as he leaned against the door frame.

"What happened to knocking?" I asked.

"I didn't want to miss my chance."

I shook my head at him.

"The water's already off, and you're already dressed. I'd say you missed it."

"I'm not so sure."

His gaze started to dip lower.

I quickly stepped toward him and lifted my lips for a kiss. He didn't disappoint. Before I lost all sense, I wrapped the towel around myself, freeing my hands and hiding the burn.

He groaned against my lips and gently pulled back.

"As much as I want to continue, there's another reason I came in here."

"Oh?"

"Adira just called. The Council met and discussed what we told them. The fact that there was nothing to link Nicolette to any of the murders and the fact that the hooded man spoke to both of the trolls changes nothing. The Council still wants us to continue to investigate Nicolette."

A tingle of anger ran through me.

"What did they say about the hooded man?" I asked.

"If we want to pursue that lead, we can. But Nicolette remains our priority."

"Why aren't they taking his connection to the deaths seriously?"

"Because they're more afraid of Nicolette."

"Why?"

"She's the most powerful succubus out there."

I recalled Eliana saying something along those lines as well.

"Fine. Let's clear Nicolette so we can go after the other guy."

"And then we head to St. Louis for answers," he said firmly.

"Agreed."

His gaze trailed over my face.

"Need any help getting dressed?"

"This whole waiting thing is going to be a real struggle for you, isn't it?" I said with a smirk.

"You have no idea."

He kissed me hard and left me breathless in the bathroom, wondering why we were waiting in the first place. Right. Baby chickens.

After closing the door, I quickly dressed and brushed out my hair while thinking of Eliana. What would she do when she found out the Council was after her mom? Probably freak out and think the Council's actions were an indication of how badly everyone viewed Eliana's species. That was not a good thing for someone already down about who she was.

I hung up my towel and went out to the living room where Oanen was waiting.

"We need to hurry up, find Nicolette, find the cloaked crusader, and get to grandma's house."

Worry filled his gaze and he strode toward me.

"What happened? Did you pass out again?" He gently touched my cheek. "You're less pale than yesterday. I thought you were better."

I reached up and closed my hand around his.

"It's not me. It's Eliana. What do you think is going to happen when she finds out her mom is a suspect? She's sad and misses us already. I just want to hurry up so we can be there for her when she needs us most."

His gaze warmed.

"I agree. Which is why I already made plans to track down Nicolette tonight."

"Tonight? Let's go now."

His lips twitched.

"Where we need to go, they won't let us in dressed like we are."

"Where do we need to go?"

"La Fatiata Torbeni's, a high-end restaurant that caters to humans and non-humans alike if they have the money."

"Um…do we have the money?"

"We do, courtesy of the Council. Enough for a nice dinner and the clothes necessary to get in. Ready for breakfast and a day of shopping?"

I made a face.

"I think you're confusing me with Eliana. I only buy new clothes when the ones I own are falling off of me."

A wicked gleam entered his gaze, and I held up my hand in a very Oanen-like move.

"Let's pretend I didn't say that last part. Feed me, and I'll go shopping."

I EXAMINED the price tag and almost gagged.

"Who pays this much for a dress?" I asked myself.

Lifting my head, I scanned the store for Oanen and found him sitting in the lounge on the other side of the room. One of the female attendants was offering him a drink. It had been the same when we'd stopped at the suit place. While Oanen was being measured, one of the male attendants had brought me a glass of champagne and offered a shoulder massage. For a moment, I'd thought the guy had been hitting on me. But he'd done the same for the next woman who'd walked in with her husband. Given the fact I'd been drugged by bacon and that Oanen had a hard time with me receiving any male attention, I'd declined both the drink and the massage.

However, Oanen seemed to have no problem accepting his champagne and shoulder rub.

Narrowing my eyes at the woman, I turned my back to them and continued browsing through dresses. I was out of my element. They all looked fancy to me. But so did the black lacy dress that I owned.

I took my phone out and dialed Eliana.

Since it was in the middle of school, I didn't expect her to pick up on the third ring.

"Hey, Megan," she said breathlessly.

"Hey. Are you okay?"

"Yeah, I just ran out of General Living Skills."

"You didn't need to do that. I could have left a voicemail."

"Are you kidding? It's General Living Skills. I know how to live with humans. The class is a waste of my time. What's up? Why'd you call?"

"I'm hoping you can help me pick out a dress. It's supposed to be for a super fancy restaurant. Think high class, not hooker."

Eliana sniggered.

"Turn on video chat and show me the options."

I did as she asked and panned the dresses.

"Grab the red one, the gold one, and that lavender one. Those colors will look good on you."

Each dress had a plunging neckline. I turned the phone around, already shaking my head.

"Those won't work. I have a bruise," I said vaguely, knowing Oanen could probably hear, "and need something with a higher neckline.

"Okay. Show me again."

She picked three different ones, which would cover the burns on my front and my back. I went to grab them from the racks, but Eliana stopped me.

"No, no, no. You wave one of the attendants over. They handle the dresses while showing you to a fitting room. Send me pics of each one front and back so I can tell you which works. I better get back to class."

"Thank you," I said quickly.

Pocketing my phone, I looked toward the attendant hovering around Oanen. When I caught her attention, I waved her over. The woman took the dresses and showed me to a changing room. I dutifully sent a picture of myself in each dress to Eliana.

She chose the one in rose gold and gave me the strict order to pair it with large diamond stud earrings and a soft updo because of the high neckline. I smirked as I typed up my response.

*What exactly does an up do?*

*You're hopeless. When you get home, we're going shopping for a week so I can be assured you'll not go out looking like a frump.*

*Frump? When did my grandma get here?*

*I'm texting Oanen that I need a picture before you walk out the door.*

Grinning, I stepped out of the changing room once again in my everyday clothes. A giggle across the store drew my attention. Both of the women were again hovering around Oanen, each rubbing a shoulder. I might not have bird hearing, but the way the one was leaning forward and trying to give Oanen a view of her cleavage hit me right between the eyes with the rage stick.

Oanen stood quickly and strode toward me, capturing my face between his hands and blocking my view of the two women I needed to kill.

"Let go," I said between clenched teeth.

"This wasn't intentional, but perhaps you now understand how I felt every time I saw Fenris touching you."

I scowled up at him.

"Fenris is a friend. One I trust not to push that boundary. Miss Hotstuff, here, is a ho who wants to ride your man-stick." He kept my face firmly between his hands, and I knew why when I saw a flicker of orange glow cast on his face.

"You're the only one who gets to ride me, Megan. Now and forever. And, unlike you, I love every ounce of jealousy you're displaying. However, we might want to make it a little less public."

I huffed out a breath.

"Would you like to purchase that dress?" a female voice asked.

My gaze narrowed.

Oanen bent his head and kissed me swiftly with so much passion that the room spun. I clutched at his shoulders and returned his kiss with every bit of need I felt for him. When he pulled away, I could only blink stupidly at his handsome face.

"Yes, we want the dress," Oanen said without looking away from me. He tugged it out of my arms and handed it off before returning to my lips.

"God, she is so lucky. What I wouldn't give for an hour alone with him."

The whisper snapped me out of the moment, and I jerked away from Oanen.

He didn't release me.

"I'm blinded by you, Megan" he said. "Struck senseless. There isn't a sunrise or sunset that can compare to the beauty of your eyes. Or any temptation that could lure me away from the chance of a moment in your welcoming arms. There is only you."

I sighed in defeat.

"You win. There will be no maiming today."

"I'd like to guarantee that."

"How?"

"Close your eyes and let me carry you out of here."

"I bought a ridiculously priced dress and need diamond stud earrings the size of my pinky nails to go with it. Since I'm dressing like a diva, I might as well act like one. Go ahead and carry me out to the car, bird boy."

He grinned, and I closed my eyes as he bent to pick me up.

"You bitches better not be looking at his backside," I called over my shoulder as he walked out the door.

He chuckled and paused long enough for two bags to be set on my stomach. Thankfully, they didn't touch my front burn.

I waited to speak until the sound of traffic indicated we were outside again.

"So where am I going to go buy earrings?" I asked.

"Nowhere. Eliana will pick something from her jewelry and have Adira leave it in the apartment before we get home."

I opened my eyes to peer up at him.

"She also demanded a picture, stating, and I quote, 'No friend of mine can show up at La Fatiata Torbeni's looking like a hobo.'"

"Jeans and t-shirts do not make me a hobo."

"This is not a battle I will ever win. Talk to Eliana."

"Chicken."

"Nope. Griffin. But I hear there's a close family resemblance when we're young."

I snorted and held the bags as he opened the door and deposited me inside. Despite the bustling sidewalks and busy shops, only a few wisps of wicked distracted me from my perusal of Oanen's backside as he walked around the car.

"It's not the same, you know," I said when he got in. "Your jealousy and mine."

"How is that?"

"I could see that woman wanted to get into your pants. Fenris didn't want to get into mine."

"I'm still not sure about that."

I snorted.

"Trust me, he has no interest in me that way. At all."

"He sure made it seem that way."

Annoyed, I lifted my phone and typed out a quick message to Fenris.

*Enough's enough. I'm telling him.*

*I understand. But promise you'll keep him away from Uttira for at least 3 weeks afterward so he cools down.*

*Deal.*

I turned slightly in my seat and faced Oanen.

"I'll tell you why Fenris acted the way he did, but you have to swear to me that once I tell you, you won't do anything to hurt Fenris physically, mentally, or emotionally."

Oanen's expression closed off.

"Tell me."

"Promise me."

"I promise I won't do anything until we're home."

"And you won't go home without me?"

"No. We stick together."

"Okay then. Fenris likes Eliana."

Oanen frowned a little and glanced at me.

"That doesn't deny the possibility of him having interest in you, too. You've seen how he is with females. He likes them all."

I made a face.

"I think it's a bigger deal than Fenris is letting on. Remember how he loved hugging me? He was doing it to smell Eliana on me. Like a lot. And when I found out that you were into me because of this whole mate and bonding thing and freaked out, Fenris came into the kitchen when I was boiling hot and burned himself to calm me down. And why did he risk himself like that? Because Eliana was worried. It had nothing to do with me. It was all about her. The level of interest he was showing..." I shrugged. "I don't know anything about this mate run. But, I know Fenris said something about once a werewolf catches a scent that he finds irresistible, he won't let up. I think Fenris' irresistible is Eliana."

Oanen's grip on the steering wheel tightened, and I heard the leather crackle.

I reached over and set my hand on his leg.

"I can't think of anyone better for Eliana than Fenris."

"In what world is that leg-humper good enough for Eliana?"

I grinned at his brotherly sentiment.

"In the world where a succubus is afraid of anything sexual. Fenris is waiting for her, Oanen. He's giving her space and time. He's fighting every single urge he has. If that doesn't mean he's good enough for her, I don't know what does."

Oanen let out a long breath, and his grip relaxed slightly.

"Does she know?"

"No. Just like you swore Eliana to secrecy, Fenris swore me to secrecy. He thinks if she knows, she'd freak out even more."

Oanen nodded.

"We need to resolve the troll deaths and your sickness then get back to Uttira."

"About that. I promised that I'd keep you out of Uttira for the next three weeks."

"I thought you said you wanted to hurry up and get back for Eliana."

"Yes, I do. You, however, need to stay out of her and Fenris' business, and I don't think you're going to if you're nearby. Maybe you'd be willing to let me stay in Uttira while you're out on enforcer business?"

He held up a hand to stall me from saying anything else. "Let's worry about that when we return to Uttira later. Right now, we have more important things to worry about."

"Like what?"

"Like our first real dinner date."

My stomach did a happy dance.

Several hours, multiple Eliana calls, and a dozen makeup tutorials later, I emerged from the apartment bathroom, dressed and ready for a late dinner at La Fatiata Torbeni's.

I nervously smoothed my hands down my skirt and gave myself one more sweeping glance. The high neckline of the floor-length dress circled my neck, covering my burns but leaving my shoulders bare. The strings of material that ran down my sides to connect the front and back didn't cover much at all. Between the delicate cross lacings, my skin showed from the side of my breast all the way to my hip.

Even with so much exposed, the dress had class. The earrings and softly upswept hair helped.

I looked amazing. But, for how long? Even though my temper had been quiet, I worried that tonight it would rear its ugly head.

"Don't screw this up, Megan. One busted lacing and you'll look like you're wearing a loincloth," I warned myself in the mirror before turning away to leave the bedroom.

At the sound of the door opening, Oanen stopped his pacing in the living room and turned to look at me.

He said nothing as I did a slow turn with my arms a little raised.

"Breathtaking," he finally said.

"You're not so bad yourself."

He was positively mouthwatering. The dark suit fit him to perfection, accentuating his golden good looks. The increasing amber flooding into his eyes created a warm pool in my middle.

If we kept staring hungrily at each other, I knew what would happen whether I thought myself ready or not.

"Ready to feed me?" I asked.

He offered his arm and escorted me from the apartment.

I wasn't going to lie to myself; I felt like a damn princess. But in a good way.

Oanen couldn't stop glancing at me all the way to the restaurant, which was a great distraction from the annoyance crawling under my skin.

When we arrived, more than one well-dressed patron glanced my way. With all the flattering male attention, it was hard to remember why we were there.

The Maître D led us to the high-ceilinged dining room and pulled out my chair for me. Oanen waved him away. I smiled and let Oanen help me sit. Not that I needed it. When I was appropriately seated, his fingers brushed the back of my neck.

"I wish we would have stayed home," he said close to my ear.

I shivered, and he chuckled before taking his own seat.

A server brought us leather-bound portfolios; and

another server appeared with a green bottle, which he opened with a flourish and poured into two glasses for us. All the while, the first one spoke in low tones about the chef's two menu options for the night.

"We'll need a few moments," I said when he stopped talking and looked at me expectantly.

He walked away, and I glanced at Oanen.

"What the hell kind of place is this?"

"The kind that requires a suit jacket, doesn't put prices on the menu, and caters to everyone."

I opened the menu and saw he was right. I also saw that I didn't understand half of what was on the fancy paper.

"Is this in English?"

"Yes. Most of it. Why?"

"The only English bits I understand are eel, sole, and tuna. I'm going to starve."

"The chef is amazing. Give the food a chance."

"You weren't almost eaten by an overgrown fish. Several of them. I don't think I'll ever be able to eat seafood again."

"There's a duckling with fig sauce."

"Perfect." I snapped my menu shut, and the server returned immediately.

A burst of sultry feminine laughter drew my attention to the other side of the room while Oanen ordered for us. A large table of seven men and one familiar female dined there. Nicolette leaned toward the man on her left and gave him a long kiss while the rest watched wistfully.

Our server moved away, and I looked at Oanen.

"Now what?"

"Now we enjoy our meal. As long as she's sitting there,

there's nothing for us to do. When she leaves, we'll follow and see what we learn."

For the next hour and a half, we did just that. Course after artistically displayed tiny course, we consumed our meal and speculated about when Elbner and Piepen would arrive in Uttira, how long I'd enjoy a rainbow-colored house, where we'd travel when everything was done, and how I wouldn't try to kill the chef for tucking a chunk of raw tuna into an innocent looking ball of crumbs.

After all our plates were cleared, Oanen came around to help me stand again.

"Where are we going?" I asked, flicking my gaze at Nicolette's table. They were still drinking wine and eating their meal.

As I watched, a well-dressed older man approached their group from the bar area. Nicolette smiled seductively as he leaned down to say something to her.

Her sultry laugh rang out in the room again.

"I'm sure you would taste divine, but I enjoy youth over experience."

The comment only further confirmed that Nicolette wouldn't have gone after an old troll.

Oanen set my hand on his arm and guided me out of the restaurant into the cold winter evening and quickly helped me into his car. Positioned to watch the entrance, he started the engine but didn't pull away from the curb.

He reached into the back and wrapped a soft cream-colored blanket around me.

"Where did this come from?"

"The apartment. I wasn't sure how long we'd need to wait tonight," he said.

"You heard Nicolette when we left, right?" I said.

"Yes."

"There's zero link here. We need to call the Council."

"We can try." He dialed Adira's number and put her on speaker phone.

"Have you followed her home?" Adira asked.

"Not yet. She's still in the restaurant."

"Adira, I don't think she's the killer. She's into young men. There's nothing linking her to any of the troll deaths. And, I don't sense anything around her. If she were a killer, wouldn't my fury be going crazy?"

The line was quiet for a long moment.

"Have you passed out again?" she asked. "Since the gas station?"

I looked up at Oanen and gave him a dirty look.

"What does that have to do with anything?" I paused and frowned. "Do you know something I should know?"

"Fury," she said respectfully, "I know many things that you do not know. But I doubt any of it would help you. It is the belief of the Council that Nicolette is guilty regardless of what you currently sense. Notify me when you have her subdued, and I will retrieve her."

Adira disconnected the call.

"Subdued? What in the hell does that mean?"

"It means I need to fight Eliana's pregnant mom."

# CHAPTER NINE

"THE COUNCIL IS SO STUPID. WHY CAN'T THEY SEE THERE'S NO proof that Nicolette is guilty?" I shifted in my seat, irritated.

"They see it," Oanen said, not looking away from the door, "but they don't care. My guess is that they're thinking if she's not guilty yet, she soon will be."

Before I could reply, one of the men from Nicolette's group stepped out of the restaurant. He paused on the sidewalk and reached into his pocket. From down the street, a set of headlights flashed and he headed that direction. An engine purred to life a few moments after I lost sight of him.

Nicolette strolled out of the restaurant, surrounded by her entourage, as the car pulled up in front of her. Her gaze swept over the street, and Oanen quickly turned his head toward me.

"Don't let her see your face," he said softly.

I shifted slightly so his head blocked me from Nicolette's view.

We waited as she got into the car, and the men

disbursed to their own vehicles. It wasn't hard to follow her line of lovers to her place, a high-rise apartment in Manhattan with underground parking and a guard. Nicolette's car led the way underground. Each car after her stopped to speak to the guard.

Oanen hesitated then went around the line and parked on the street.

I looked at the building's front door where another man guarded the entrance.

"I can take him," I said with confidence.

"So could I, but we don't need to."

He shrugged out of his jacket and handed it to me. I groaned.

"I really don't like when you do this."

"Why? Because all the ladies will see my man-stick?"

"I regret ever saying that."

His lips twitched as he unbuttoned his shirt and kicked off his shoes.

"You'll need to carry my clothes," he said. "There's a bag in the back."

I twisted in my seat and grabbed a backpack laying on the backseat along with his winter jacket. His lips brushed my neck before I could straighten. My eyes closed, and I held still to enjoy the feel of him for a moment.

"What was that for?" I asked when he stopped.

"A reminder that what I feel for you is real."

"I already know that."

He exhaled slowly and looked up at the building.

"I just don't want you to forget it when we get inside Nicolette's apartment."

"I won't."

He handed me his jacket, shoes, and socks, then got out of the car. I had everything in the backpack by the time he opened my door and offered his hand.

I accepted his help and grinned when he held the bag so I could put his jacket on while he stood there barefoot in an unbuttoned shirt.

"Careful, you're only adding to my growing princess complex. I'm going to want peeled grapes next."

"I'll feed them to you tonight. Ready?" He held out his hand, and I threaded my fingers through his.

"Where are we going?" I asked as he started down the sidewalk away from the building.

"Somewhere less public."

We found a quiet place in a nearby park. Oanen led me into the trees and stepped back to strip out of the rest of his clothes. I caught everything and folded it into the backpack. When I once again had the bag on my shoulders, Oanen stood before me in his beak and feathers.

"Let's go, bird boy."

He bent a knee so I could climb on his back. The skirt of the dress didn't have enough room so I ended up bunching it around my waist. My legs prickled with the cold, and I frowned.

"Don't take too long in the air," I said as I ran my hand down his neck.

He clacked his beak and turned his head to nuzzle my bare leg. A moment later, he lunged into the air and broke free of the trees.

I would never tire of flying with Oanen. My heart soared, seeing the lights and cars below us and the stars above. I held tight as he made his way back toward Nicolette's building, circling it slowly.

"There," I said, pointing to a balcony at the top.

The French doors were open, and the apartment was filled with people in various stages of undress. Most of them were men. But there were a few couples doing things publicly that hinted at a succubus's playhouse.

Oanen went right for the balcony. His landing went unnoticed by the couple on the lounge.

Averting my gaze from the man's naked backside as he rapidly thrust into his moaning partner, I slid off Oanen and dug in the bag for his pants.

He put them on quickly, while keeping his gaze on me.

"It's likely to get worse," he said quietly.

The sound of skin against skin almost drowned out his words.

"How can it get worse than this?"

The woman started yelling, "Yes, yes, yes!" at the top of her lungs then wailed in rapture. My cheeks heated, and my legs no longer felt so cold.

I waited for the couple to notice us as Oanen put on his shirt then socks. But they didn't. Instead, they started up again.

I stared at Oanen in shock.

"We can't feel it, but what they're doing is giving off sexual energy. It's what nourishes a succubus," he said softly. "With Nicolette being pregnant, she'll be hungrier than a typical succubus. Like I said, it'll be worse inside. Are you ready?"

Now fully dressed and with the empty bag over his shoulder, Oanen held out his hand to me.

I swallowed hard and nodded. Together, we walked inside.

A man holding a tray of champagne walked our way. He wasn't wearing a thing except a bow tie.

"These formal affairs are amazing, don't you agree?" he said, giving me a heated look.

Oanen's fingers tightened around mine.

"Incredible," I said with a smile. "Can you point us toward our hostess?"

The man nodded toward the center of the room and walked away with a wink.

"Do not leave my side," Oanen warned.

"I won't."

We moved in the direction the server had indicated, weaving our way through people, until we saw the pile of pillows in the center of the room. People lay on the cushions. While there was an obvious imbalance of men to women, the few women there didn't seem to mind that they were being petted by several men at once.

I tried to focus on Nicolette, who lounged in the center of it all, sipping a glass of green liquid. Her black gaze flicked from one pile of sweaty bodies to the next.

"I think Paulette would be more comfortable on all fours," she said to the group on her left.

The men immediately moved away from the woman so she could change position. A molten heat filled my face as one man knelt behind Paulette and another lay down under her.

"Much better," Nicolette said.

Even if Oanen wasn't in over his head in all of this, I

sure was. I nudged him, desperate for him to do whatever he needed, so we could get the hell out of there.

The move caught Nicolette's attention, and her gaze flicked to us.

"Aren't you two just adorable," she said. "Are you here to have some fun?"

"No," I said quickly.

"We're here on behalf of the Council," Oanen said. "They would like to speak with you."

"Really?" Her amused tone was gone. "I think not."

She stood in one smooth move, her dress shimmering in the light.

"I think you're here to satisfy some urges, Oanen. Look at her." Nicolette's voice turned sultry. "Her pretty eyes. Deep pools pleading with you to end her longing."

Oanen turned to look at me, his eyes already a deep gold.

"Oanen?" I said, hesitantly as he dropped the bag.

"Megan." His voice was a rough rasp as he caressed my cheek. "Be strong for both of us," he said a moment before his lips crashed upon mine.

I trembled under the intensity of his kiss.

"That's right," Nicolette cooed. "You have so much suppressed passion for each other. Let it free."

A heat pooled in my stomach and drifted lower. I threaded my hands in Oanen's hair and kissed him back with as much passion as he kissed me.

"Bring her to the cushions, my darling Oanen. And remove your shirt so she can touch you."

His lips didn't leave mine as he picked me up and moved us. But they did when he removed his shirt.

Panting, I stared up at the golden expanse of his chest. I wanted to touch him. To run my tongue over every ridge and dip. I wanted to fill myself with Oanen and to be filled by him.

"Megan, my dear. I think that beautiful dress is in his way. Take it off."

The heat surged. I wanted to be under Oanen. Naked. Waiting. Exposed.

I blinked.

Exposed?

My gaze shifted from Oanen's loving face to those of the people around us. Even as part of me knew that what was happening was wrong, my fingers found the clasp at my neck.

"The Council wants you to go to Uttira," I said, unhooking the back.

"Focus, my love. Bare your breasts to him. Let him taste you."

My skin heated further, and a tingle started between my legs. But something changed. A spark ignited in my chest. Anger. My fury didn't like that it was being forced to do something that wasn't its own choice.

"Don't you understand?" I asked, fighting the urge to slip the top of the dress over my arms. Oanen's gaze tracked the material as it started to lower. I swallowed hard.

"I understand that you're trying to fight this. Don't. You both want it."

Oanen's hand found my leg under my skirt. Slowly, he skimmed his way up to my knee.

"The Council has kept you out of Uttira. Away from Eliana. Now, they want you there."

Oanen paused, his hand on my inner thigh, his fingers skimming the line of my panties.

I began to burn. Two ends of a Megan candle. One passion. The other rage. Around us the couples continued with their public orgy in earnest. The gasps and groans of pleasure weren't helping me maintain my focus.

"Eliana won't have a say whether or not you stay this time," I said. "You'll finally be with your daughter."

The black in Nicolette's gaze faded.

"You're smart," she said. "And also very resistant. It could have been fun."

Nicolette snapped her fingers.

"Finish and leave."

The sex around us turned frenzied. I gazed up at Oanen. The look in his eyes was as tormented as it was hopeful. I gently withdrew his hand from under my skirt, gave it a pat, and righted my dress, doing my best to ignore the escalating, screaming pleasure.

Everything slowly quieted and people picked up their clothes on their way to the door. One man in particular drew my attention. Like most males here, he was young, lean, and naked. However, he was also wicked as hell. A new kind of tingle started under my skin.

"You like the naughty ones?" Nicolette asked, watching me.

"No. Not at all."

When I turned toward her, orange reflected on her skin, and black briefly consumed her eyes before disappearing.

"Be careful with displays of power, Fury. Some of us can't help but rise to a challenge." She looked at Oanen. "Call your parents. I'm ready."

His hands shook as he retrieved his phone from his pants and dialed a number.

"We have her," he said then hung up.

Nicolette laughed. "You don't have anything fledgling. But, you almost did."

She winked at me just as a portal appeared beside Oanen. Adira stepped through and held out her hand to Nicolette.

"See you soon, darlings," Nicolette said before she ignored Adira and stepped through the portal on her own.

Adira looked at us.

"You don't look well, Megan."

"Don't even try to say I look pale because I know my face is on fire after what I witnessed here."

"No. It's not that. It's in your eyes. They're missing their spark."

"Well, it's been an exhausting night. I think I'm allowed to be non-sparky."

She dipped her head in acknowledgment then disappeared.

Alone in Nicolette's plush apartment, I glanced at Oanen's flushed face as he finished buttoning his shirt. Guilt laced his expression.

"Your fighting skills need improvement," I said.

"Megan, I—"

"Your make-out skills are A plus, though."

His lips twitched, and he picked up the empty bag and reached for my hand. Threading my fingers through his, we left Nicolette's apartment and waited for the elevator together. I could still feel the tremble in his hand.

"Are you okay?" I asked.

"No. I'm still fighting the urge to carry you back to the cushions and slide that dress off of you."

"I'm sorry she did that to you."

He turned toward me, the dilated pupils in his golden eyes making my pulse skip.

"That was me, Megan. She barely nudged me to do what I've been dying to do…what I've been holding back. My fingers are desperate to feel the soft skin of your thighs again. Tell me you're ready, and I'll stop fighting this."

Hearing that didn't fill me with fear. But as much as I wanted to say yes, I couldn't.

"I want our first time together to be special, not on some well-used cushions in a succubus's playhouse. And not in the middle of a murder investigation."

He closed his eyes, taking a deep breath.

"Are you mad?" I asked.

"Never. You're right. Now isn't the time. This isn't what I want to remember, either."

When he opened his eyes, there was more blue than gold in them.

"Let's go home," he said.

The elevator finally dinged and opened for us.

"You mean back to the apartment, right? We both know that Nicolette isn't the killer. We need to find the hooded man."

He nodded and pushed the button for the first floor.

"Back to the apartment. We'll start again tomorrow."

He studied me for a long moment.

"Adira's right. Your eyes are different. There was something more to them before. A warmth. A hidden fire before they ever started glowing orange. I don't see it now."

Damn Adira for bringing it up.

"Maybe my eyes changed when my power did."

"Maybe. Maybe we should forget about this hooded man, since the Council doesn't care, and leave for St. Louis first thing in the morning."

"No way. We can't do that to Eliana. She's going to freak out when she finds out her mom is in Uttira because of me."

"No. Her mom is there because of the Council and will be under Council custody," Oanen said.

I shook my head and looked at the polished door.

"I don't know about that. The Council isn't stupid. Annoying, yes. Stubborn, yes. But not stupid. There's too much evidence to say Nicolette didn't do it. So why bring her back to Uttira? There's obviously something else going on there that they aren't telling us."

Another thought occurred to me.

"Text Adira and say that we're choosing not to pursue the hooded man and see what she says," I said.

The elevators opened up to the lobby, and we stepped out. The night man at the door opened it for us and said nothing as we left.

Oanen sent a quick text off after we were settled into the car then drove us home. There was a response by the time we reached our building.

"They want us to follow up on our lead," he said.

"That's what I thought."

We walked inside, and I veered for the elevator.

Oanen frowned at me. "Are you sure you're okay?"

"I'm wearing heels. All of me is fine, except my feet, at the thought of climbing all those stairs."

While standing by the elevator door, Oanen kissed my temple and wrapped an arm around my shoulders as we watched the floors count down. The doors opened, and Oanen stepped back, guiding me with him. If he hadn't, I wouldn't have moved.

My Fury reared its head. But it felt different this time. The compulsion to yell at the guys stepping out of the elevator was there as was the anger. However, the power felt unreachable, somehow. My lips ached with the need to call out a man's name. To demand his confession. My fingers twitched to grab his neck as he obliviously strode past me.

Oanen guided me forward. My steps were slow, each one harder than the last because it was taking me further away from the man.

"Are you okay?" Oanen asked, already reaching to press the button for our floor.

The urge to strike out and slap his hand away road me hard, creating a physical ache on my hip. I frowned as the ache turned into a burn.

The door closed, blocking the man from me and snapping the draw on my power. I almost wilted in relief.

"I'm fine. Just tired."

I was more than tired. I was ready to fall to the floor. More than that. I knew I was running out of time.

THE WEIGHT of Oanen's arm pinned me to the mattress. Warm and comfortable, I could have slept forever.

However, the phone ringing near my head insisted that wasn't an option.

I reached out and swatted in the direction of the sound. My fingers hit something, and I heard a thump on the floor a moment later. Everything went quiet.

Oanen's phone started to ring next.

"I think it's unavoidable," he said before kissing my covered shoulder and rolling out of bed.

Without opening my eyes, I listened to his rough "hello."

"Yeah. She's right here. Hold on."

The mattress moved as he leaned toward me.

"It's Eliana," he said. "She's upset."

I rubbed my hand over my face and opened my eyes but didn't move from my side-sleeping position. Everything hurt just like each time I woke up after trying to send someone to hell. Only this time, it was a little less intense. As much as I wanted to take that as a good sign, I had a feeling it was because I hadn't actually acted out what my fury wanted last night.

Taking the phone from Oanen, I set it against my ear.

"Hey, Eliana."

"My mom's here," she said. I could hear the panic and anger in her voice.

"I know. And I'm sorry for my part in that. Oanen and I have been telling the Council that we don't think she had anything to do with what's going on."

Eliana snorted.

"Of course she doesn't. She doesn't kill; she just destroys lives." She made a sound of annoyance. "Stop touching yourself when you're on my bed. I saw that smear on my pillow this morning, and you're lucky I didn't kill you in my sleep."

"Uh…Eliana?"

"Sorry. Piepen and Elbner arrived last night. Elbner's at your place with his honey-milk. Piepen's here."

"That's great."

"No. It's not."

I could hear a door close.

"He's in a horny, adolescent phase and keeps touching himself. While on my pillow. Brownie lust does not taste like you'd think. You need to get your butt home as soon as possible. The brownie and my mom both need to go. Mom's staying here, Megan. At the Quills'. She's already found my stash of chocolate and eaten half of it. Once the chocolate's gone, she's going to turn her attention on me. She already commented that I look underfed."

I could hear a tapping in the background.

"I told you, I need privacy while I'm in the bathroom," Eliana said. "If you can't respect that, we'll need to find you somewhere else to stay while Megan's away."

She lowered her voice.

"I caught him showering in the run off from my pubic hairs this morning. When I went to kick him, he thanked me for the view of my flower."

As much as I hurt, I couldn't stop my laughter.

"This isn't funny, Megan. It's traumatizing. Help me. No one sees my flower. Ever!"

I bit my lip and struggled for control as Oanen watched me.

"I am helping. I swear. We're going to follow up on a lead we have that links someone else to the trolls' deaths."

"Who?"

"We don't know his name. He's just a hooded man who talked to the victims at the Goose and Gizzard before they died."

"Piepen mentioned a nice man who helped his grandparents find peace. Maybe it's the same guy."

"Maybe. Talk to Piepen and see if you can get anything useful out of him. A name. An address. What the hell the guy looks like."

"I will. Just hurry."

I heard the door open on Eliana's end before she yelled.

"Put down my underwear!"

Then, the line disconnected.

I HANDED THE PHONE BACK TO OANEN AND CAREFULLY SAT UP.

"Eliana's freaking out just like I said she would. It's not bad enough that the Council wanted Nicolette in Uttira. They put her in your house with Eliana."

Oanen frowned.

"As if that's not stressful enough for her, the brownie I sent her way is masturbating on Eliana's pillow and sneaking into the shower with her. We need to figure out who this hooded guy is fast."

"All right. Let's get dressed."

I stood too quickly and had to reach for the nightstand to steady myself.

"What's wrong?" Oanen was at my side in an instant.

"Nothing. Just got a little dizzy from standing up too fast."

"You're pale." He reached out to touch my forehead, but I swatted his hand away.

"I'm also annoyed that people keep telling me that. You can change in the bathroom. I'll change out here."

He studied me for a long moment then grabbed some clothes and closed himself in the bathroom. I hurried to get dressed, glancing at the new burn on my hip. It wasn't as severe as the others but still served as a reminder that we needed answers. Today.

Ten minutes later, we stepped outside, and I looked up at the clear sky.

"How late is it?" I asked.

"Almost noon."

"Wow." It hadn't felt like we'd slept that long.

"Are you hungry?"

"Not really."

He gave me a considering look then opened the car door for me.

Neither of us spoke during the ride to the Goose and Gizzard. I didn't mind the quiet. I closed my eyes and drifted off. When the car slowed, though, I jerked awake.

Oanen parked and cut the engine but stopped me before I got out.

"I know you don't like me asking if you're all right. You probably hate hearing it as much as I hate asking it. I just wish you'd be honest with me and tell me what's going on. I know something isn't right."

"It's more than something. It's everything. Dead trolls. Nicolette. The Council. My mom. My great-grandma. I'm sorry I'm not myself lately."

He continued to study me.

"That's not it. Or at least not all of it. If you're not ready to confide in me, that's fine. But whether you tell me or not, it won't change what will happen if you get worse. You're mine, Megan. Mine to love. To care for. To protect. Even from your stubborn self."

"Got it."

He leaned toward me and gently stroked my cheek.

"And that's how I know whatever is happening is getting very serious. Megan Smith does not simply say, 'Got it.' Ever."

He had me there. But I was too tired to argue.

"Are we going inside, or do you plan to play with my face all day?" I asked.

He kissed me lightly then reached across me to open the door.

"After you."

I felt more than a little guilty as I got out then waited for him on the sidewalk. He did have my best interest at heart. Yet, if I told him what was happening, I was worried what his plan B would be if we talked to my great-grandma and she didn't have any answers. I needed my own plan B before I said anything. Besides, things weren't as bad as my mom made it sound like they were going to be. I'd successfully managed to avoid trying to condemn someone to hell and reduced the effects of the backlash. I could hold out long enough to find the troll killer and come up with a backup plan for saving myself.

No problem.

A little, pessimistic inner voice laughed its ass off at that thought.

Inside the Gizzard, a few patrons already sat at the bar.

"No eating anything," Oanen warned before moving off to talk to a very large, ugly woman sitting by herself in one of the booths.

I went to the bar and sat beside the man there. The bartender looked at me, shook his head, then approached.

"What can I get you?"

"A soda. Any human kind," I ordered even though I had no intention of consuming any of it.

The bartender made a noise that suggested he thought I was stupid and moved off.

The man beside me gave a longsuffering sigh.

"Human drinks. Bah. I miss drinking from them. Biting into their juicy flesh. The coppery taste of their blood coating my tongue."

I glanced at the weathered old man, wondering what type of creature he might be. No matter what kind, I should have felt some fury rage right then. He'd just admitted to eating humans. Perhaps I didn't feel anything because it had happened long ago. Before the laws even. Or, perhaps the aftereffects of the burns were causing an inability to sense anything. Maybe that was what Mom meant about me being calm.

"More than that, I miss the sky," he added.

His shoulder drooped a bit more.

"My wings are shriveled and shrunken. I can barely make it from the mainland to the island anymore. Four hundred years ago, I could have flown around the world in my true form."

That admission confirmed my long time ago theory. Yet, I couldn't help but feel my other theory fit as well.

"Why not go to somewhere secluded and fly?" I asked.

He snorted.

"The humans are everywhere."

"What about going to one of the towns like Uttira? I hear we can use our true forms openly there."

He turned his craggy face toward me and scowled.

"Exchanging the freedom to fly for my freedom to roam would solve nothing. My life, the lives of all dragons, mean nothing now. This world has no place for us."

The bartender came back with a burger, which he set in front of the old man. While the old guy lifted his bun to inspect the food, the bartender poured me a glass of white soda.

"Everything okay with the burger, Magroal?" the bartender asked.

The old guy set the bun down.

"As good as ground up, old-kill animal flesh can be."

The bartender nodded and took a half-full glass from the other side of the old man and went in the back. Magroal took a huge bite of his burger, chewed methodically, and swallowed. The thing smelled amazing. Had I been eating it, I would have been making moaning noises of appreciation. Well, not here, but anywhere else that served a bacon cheeseburger.

He finished the rest of the burger in three bites, threw down some cash, and left. His fries and drink were untouched. I looked around the rest of the bar.

Oanen was still talking to the ugly girl. There was another older guy in a booth, but something about his red eyes as he glanced at me kept me in my seat.

I really was losing my edge.

My stomach rumbled, and I looked back at the remnants of old guy's meal, tempted to take a fry. I reached out and turned the plate.

"Megan," came Oanen's warning voice from across the room.

I would have turned to grin at him, but my gaze was caught on the green flecks of powder on the edge of the plate.

"Oanen, there's more powder here."

He rushed to my side. Instead of looking where I pointed, he grabbed my shoulders.

"Did you eat any?" Worry filled his expression.

"Of course not."

His gaze searched mine before he released me and looked at the plate.

The bartender walked out from the kitchen. Oanen waved him over and pointed to the powder.

"It happened again. Do you have someone in back that we can borrow?"

"Borrow?" I asked.

"We need someone to eat that so we can follow them."

"Yeah," the bartender said. "I've got someone. He needs to come back, though. He's my nephew and does the dishes."

I couldn't tell which part was more important to him. The relation to the boy or having his dishes washed.

"Tek! Get out here!"

A young man close to our age appeared from the back.

"Eat that," the bartender said.

"The fries?"

"No. The powder on the plate."

"Why? It's not from me. I know that plate was clean when you grabbed it."

"It's not a punishment. Just eat the damn shit."

The boy licked his finger, dabbed up the few granules of powder, then swiped it on his tongue. We all watched him, waiting.

"Doesn't taste like anything," the boy said after a few long moments.

"How long does it take to work?" Oanen asked.

"The guy ate his whole burger. I only managed a few bites." I shrugged. "I have no idea."

We both watched Tek.

"Work?" he asked. "What was that stuff?"

"A spell that calls you to a location, I think," Oanen said.

"You had me eat a spell, and you don't even know what it does?" Tek asked, looking a little nervous now.

Oanen ignored him and focused on the bartender.

"Who was he? The guy sitting here?"

"Magroal. A dragon. He lives on one of the islands, but I'm not sure which one."

"The Council called Raiden to sniff out a killer," I said. "Can we call him to see if he can follow Magroal's trail?"

The bartender snorted.

"In New York? Good luck."

Oanen shook his head.

"There's too many smells here. We'd never find anyone that way."

"Okay. Well, how did the powder get on the burger? Maybe we can figure out something that way."

Oanen and I went back to review the camera footage. It didn't take long to rewind the thirty minutes since we had arrived. When we did, my jaw dropped.

I watched us walk in. Oanen went to the ugly chick. I went to the bar to join the two men sitting there. Two.

Directly on the other side of the old dragon sat the hooded man.

"How?" I said. "We didn't see him."

"A powerful spell," Oanen said grimly. "He knows we're looking for him."

As we watched, the old dragon lifted his bun. The hooded man reached over and sprinkled the food while the old dragon talked to the bartender. Instead of getting up and leaving, the hooded man waited until the dragon finished the burger then got up with him and followed him out the exit.

"Wait," Oanen said, sifting through the camera angles. "There."

He paused the video frame. This time, one of the camera's had captured a clear image of the hooded man's face. He was younger, just a little older than Oanen and me. We finally had a picture of him.

I took my phone and snapped a picture.

"Time to visit the Tabernam," I said again.

We checked on Tek before leaving. He still seemed unaffected.

"Likely because of the low dose," Oanen said. "Keep an eye on him and call me if anything changes."

The bartender nodded.

Outside, Oanen hesitated on the sidewalk, glancing at me then the sky.

"I agree," I said. "You should fly and try to spot him. He can't have gotten too far."

"No, we stick together."

"I'll be fine, Oanen. I'll drive straight to the Tabernam."

"Until someone distracts you. No. We're together. Always."

I didn't argue as he continued toward the car. He was right. If my rage kicked in, I'd likely drive off the road, trying to get to whoever. But, given how I was feeling, I doubted it would happen. And that wasn't something I was going to mention to Oanen.

The drive to the Tabernam didn't take long, and when we entered the store, the woman came out from behind the counter to greet us.

"Enforcer. Fury," she said a bit too loudly. "How can I help you?"

I took out my phone and showed her a picture of the hooded man.

"Have you seen him?"

"Yes. He came in a few weeks ago. I haven't seen him since, though. And before you ask, I do not know his name or where he lives. All I can give you is a list of the ingredients he purchased."

"Good," Oanen said. "Send it to the Council. If you see him again, call the Council immediately."

"Yes, Enforcer."

Oanen nodded, and with his hand on my back, we left.

"You didn't buy that bull, did you?" I asked.

"Most of it. I think she told the truth about not knowing his name or address. But I also think she knew someone who would know it. And that someone was probably in the shop."

We sat in the car for over an hour, waiting for someone to emerge, but no one did.

"Should we go back in?"

"No. Whoever she was warning probably already left another way."

He started the car and merged with the light traffic.

"We have his picture and know he's part of the nonhuman community since he was in the Gizzard. And, he obviously knows we're looking for him already if he's using the cloaking spell. So, let's start visiting all the nonhuman secret places and asking around. Someone is bound to recognize him."

Oanen gave me a wry side glance.

"This is New York. Do you know how many places there are that cater to only non-humans? And how many more places cater to both? We'll be searching for weeks."

"Then we better get started."

ANOTHER EARLY MORNING call woke me.

"We need to leave our phones in the kitchen on silent from now on," I mumbled into my pillow.

"That wouldn't help us leave here any faster." Oanen chuckled as he left the bed to answer the call.

"Hello," he said as he walked from the room.

As much as I wanted to go back to sleep, I knew that Oanen was right. We'd spent the previous day going from place to place, showing the picture of the hooded man. At most places, no one claimed to have seen him. At a select few of the establishments, he'd been noticed, but no one knew who he was. However, I'd noticed a pattern that might help narrow our search. The hooded man liked to slum it and seemed to only visit places the old and poor would go.

Thanks to that little bit of information, Oanen and I were looking at a few days more of searching instead of a few weeks.

I got out of bed and closed myself in the bathroom. Brushing my teeth was a chore. Dark circles ringed my eyes. We'd stayed out too late, and I looked like hell for it. But I shouldn't have. All-nighters shouldn't have been affecting me at all, physically.

As I stripped for a shower, I checked the burns. They weren't looking any better.

I slipped into the water with a sigh and started washing. The door opened.

"Bad news," Oanen said. "There was another death. A dragon this time."

"Big surprise."

"It is. The death happened a few days ago, but the body was discovered this morning."

"So not the dragon from yesterday."

"Apparently not. Dress warm. We'll have to fly to this one."

The door closed, and I hurried through the rest of my shower. I was a little bummed it wasn't the dragon from the day before. Not that I wanted him to die, but if it had been him, it would have cleared Nicolette's name. I didn't trust the Council's reason for keeping Nicolette in Uttira.

However, clearing Eliana's mom's name wouldn't have solved my biggest problem. I needed to figure out how to not die or kill Grandma Irene before we went to talk to her.

Thankfully, my hope that we'd find the killer yesterday

had been too lofty. The city was big and the non-human community too suspicious. That meant I had more time. It also meant, Oanen's worry would only grow.

Oanen hadn't mentioned it when I'd started yawning by eight last night. He'd only stopped at a corner store, like I'd asked, to grab some breakfast food so we wouldn't need to keep going out. I didn't mind eating at restaurants, but I didn't want to waste any more time than necessary…more for Eliana's sake than my own.

Fifteen minutes and a bowl of cereal later, I stood on the balcony, Oanen's clothes already in the bag on my back. He shifted quickly and dipped a knee.

"You make me nervous when you skip breakfast," I said climbing on.

He twisted his head to look at me.

"I'm worried a random rabbit is going to distract you mid-flight." He clacked his beak at me and bit the cuff of my jeans. I grinned.

"Come on, bird boy, before you get any hungrier."

The feathers around his neck ruffled a bit before he leapt into the air with enough force to make me squeal.

The flight to the island didn't take long. Seated between two bodies of water, the place was big enough for a few buildings but was lush with greenery instead. Oanen circled, dropping lower with each pass. On the third one, we were low enough for me to see bits of cement and steel in the green. He landed on top of a building that had a large hole in its roof.

I hesitated to get off when Oanen bent his leg.

"I better not fall through," I said. "I have a feeling falling into this building would be as nasty as falling into a lake."

He tugged on my pant leg with his beak, and I slid off. He shifted to his skin and crossed his arms, giving me his pre-lecture look.

"You are not allowed to lecture naked. It's too distracting," I said tossing the bag at him and turning my back.

"You think I'd hunt a rabbit with you on my back?" he asked.

"Ew. You'd actually eat a raw rabbit," I teased as I listened to him zip his pants.

"A little bit of cereal in your belly," he said close to my ear, "and you're nothing but trouble."

I turned and lightly kissed him.

"You like me this way."

"I do." He wrapped his arms around me and kissed me more firmly before pulling away.

I shivered lightly, and it had nothing to do with his toe-curling kiss.

"Let's get you inside."

He led me to the roof exit and opened the door.

"The hole isn't real," he said. "You should have felt the tingle of magic when we landed."

I cringed, but he didn't say anything else, and that worried me more than any lecture.

Inside, the building looked fairly nice. Much better than either trolls' place.

We walked down the well-lit flight of stairs to the hall.

"Third door on the left," Oanen said.

I followed him to the open door and stopped short at the smell. Oanen frowned slightly and walked further into the room. I covered my nose and mouth with my hand and stepped in behind him.

The man lay on his couch, his prone pose peaceful. The serene smile on his face seemed out of place. Probably because of the scowl lines between his eyes.

"He's been dead several days for sure," Oanen said pulling back the man's sleeve and looking at the darkened underside of his arm.

I looked around the room while he continued to inspect the body. Every piece of furniture looked old. Really old. But all well cared for. I didn't know much about antiques, but the pieces seemed like they were from different eras.

"I don't get it," I said, my sleeve muffling my words. "Why go from killing trolls to killing a dragon? Other than being all males and dying with a smile, there's no pattern."

"No pattern that we're seeing," Oanen said.

My sleeve stopped working, and I gagged.

"I'll be on the roof," I said, backing up a step.

Oanen's gaze pinned me, and he opened his mouth. However, whatever he saw when he looked at me had his expression changing.

"I won't be long. Stay on the roof, and keep the door open so I can hear you. A little fresh air will do this place some good."

I nodded and fled before I threw up all over the crime scene.

CHAPTER ELEVEN



"Are you sure you're okay?" Eliana asked, yet again.

"I'm fine. You would have sounded breathless and shaky, too, if you'd inhaled a whiff of four-day old dead dragon."

My stomach rolled sickeningly.

"It's a smell I'm never going to forget. I don't know how Oanen is still down there. He's going to need a shower after this."

"I like showers!" a high-pitched voice shouted in the background.

Eliana gave a long-suffering sigh.

"Please tell me you're getting closer to figuring out who really did this."

"I wish I could. It would have been great if this dragon was freshly dead."

"Uh?"

"It would have been clear evidence that your mom wasn't responsible."

"Oh, yeah. Well, not that I'm wishing for any fresh deaths, but you're right. It would have been convenient."

"How's it going? Is she being a good mom?"

"Absolutely. She's the perfect succubus mom. She brought me an assortment of toys yesterday. And I'm not talking teddy bears. Also, she assures me she'll get me a teddy immediately. Not the stuffed kind." She lowered her voice. "I'm afraid I..."

I angrily kicked at the roof's ledge when the silence grew. My hate for the Council only increased.

"I'm sure the Council would understand matricide in these circumstances," I joked, desperate to lighten her mood.

Eliana gave a weak laugh.

"I better go check on Elbner. The less I'm at home being showered by my mother's affection and sage advice, the better."

"Let me know if either he or Piepen has anything useful to say."

"I will."

When I hung up and turned around, Oanen was leaning against the door.

"Feeling better?" he asked.

"Yep."

He took a step toward me, and I held up a hand.

"You don't smell like him, do you?"

Oanen cocked his head and studied me, worry clouding his eyes.

"You were never this squeamish."

"Wrong. The sight of blood and gore, I can handle. Seeing

Aubrey eat someone, while gross, was no problem. Watching Trammer blow his brains out was upsetting because of Ashlyn, but not because of the graphic display. Seeing the oracle gobble mermaids whole? Well, that was just fun. But, in every one of those situations, not once was I exposed to a smell like I was in there. I'm not visually squeamish. It's all about the nose. So stop worrying, and tell me you found something that will help us figure this out faster."

"I did. He's the dragon whose burger you ate the first day here."

I frowned.

"That means he had to have run into the hooded guy again after. It's a three-day window."

"Three days of footage we already covered at the Gizzard."

"Crap. How are we supposed to find this guy?" I paced the roof for a moment. "We know the victim, have a suspect, and know the timeframe. I say we keep asking around. Only this time, we have more details."

It shouldn't have been that hard. At least, not in my way of thinking.

However, a day later, we weren't any closer to finding the hooded man.

"You're getting edgy again," Oanen observed as I tossed my hairbrush to the vanity counter.

I gave him a so-what look.

"It's close to noon, and I'm hungry."

He shook his head, not buying my explanation.

"Since coming here, you get worse after you get edgy."

I exhaled slowly and tried to ignore the annoyance that had started crawling under my skin late last night. We'd managed to stay out until three a.m. before I'd said I needed sleep.

"I'm—"

"Fine. I know." He straightened away from the doorway. "Let's go out for breakfast. We can ask around while we eat."

I nodded and followed him out of the apartment.

On the street, I could feel wisps of wicked. Nothing to set me off but enough to make me think I'd been right the day before. Whenever I got a burn, my ability to sense wickedness seemed suppressed for a while. And Oanen had noticed the pattern before I had.

The ride to the restaurant was quiet except for the ping of Oanen's phone.

"Want me to check it?" I asked.

"Nah. It can wait until after we eat."

"You think it's another dead body, don't you?"

"I do."

I reached into his pocket and withdrew his phone. He didn't try to stop me from scanning the message.

"Another dragon," I said, sliding the phone back into his pocket. "Same building as the last one." I looked out the window. "And your mom wants to know if I'm feeling any better."

"Are you mad?" he asked after a moment.

"No. I get that I'm worrying you, and I'm sorry for it."

We didn't say anything else until he pulled in front of a familiar non-human diner. Oanen caught my hand before I could reach for the door.

"Don't be sorry, Megan. Just let me help."

"You are."

I leaned forward and kissed him lightly. Worry that bordered on fear consumed me then vanished.

In that moment, I knew I was in trouble. It had nothing to do with killing my grandma or my burns but everything to do with my heart. I loved Oanen. So much that it hurt to breathe.

"You just paled."

"I'm sure I did," I said, reaching up and gently running my fingers through his hair. "You were in my head."

He closed his eyes briefly.

"I'm sorry. I didn't mean to let it slip."

"Don't be sorry for caring, Oanen." I exhaled deeply and set my head on his shoulder. "I can't wait for all of this to be over. I want to go home and paint our house rainbow colors and make the Council twitchy just for fun."

He grunted a half laugh and stroked his hand over my hair. We took comfort in each other for a silent moment before I pulled away.

"Sitting here won't make my dreams come true any faster. Let's eat so we can get to the corpse before it starts to smell."

His lips twitched, and he got out to open the door for me.

"From any other person, that statement might worry me."

I stood on my toes and pressed a quick kiss to his cheek.

"That just means I'm your kind of warped," I said.

The wisps of annoyance intensified the moment Oanen opened the diner's door for me. Playing it cool, I didn't hesitate. I went straight to an open booth and plopped down. Oanen slid in across from me and grabbed a menu from the holder. He tried to offer the single, laminated sheet to me, but I shook my head.

"I already know what I want," I said. "You sure it's okay to eat first?"

"I learned my lesson the last time we left here without feeding you. Besides, it's not like the guy's going anywhere."

The same waitress as before came to our table and set two waters down.

"I know what I want," I said before she could leave.

"All right. What can I get you?"

"Two eggs, over-easy. Bacon. A double order. Hash browns with onions and cheese. And a side order of pancakes."

"You got it." She turned her attention to Oanen without writing anything down. "You know what you want?"

"The same, please."

She nodded and went back to the kitchen.

"I'm going to ask around while we wait for our food. Don't move from this table," Oanen said.

He took his phone out and brought up the camera app, using it to scan the room. It took a second to realize he was using it to check if the hooded man was in the diner with us.

"Smart and good-looking," I said. "I might just keep you."

He winked at me and left our booth. I kept an eye on him as he went around the diner, showing the picture to the patrons. I wasn't the only one keeping tabs on Oanen, however. The waitress watched him closely, too. Hopefully, she wasn't thinking of trying to kick us out for disturbing customers or something. I wanted my food.

The phone in my pocket buzzed, and I took it out, expecting a message from Eliana. Instead, I saw my mom's number.

*Rumor is that you haven't left town yet. For your sake, those better be unfounded rumors.*

My temper flared. The old me would have been slightly cowed by this kind of message. Not the new, abandoned-and-so-over-it me.

*Your mom-card expired the day you ditched me in Uttira. Stop acting like you care now.*

I watched the phone, waiting for a reply, but none came.

Oanen slid back into the booth.

"Eliana again?" he asked.

I was saved from answering by the arrival of the waitress.

She set down our plates, and my mouth watered with anticipation. I was so focused on the food, I almost didn't catch her reaching out to place a hand on Oanen's shoulder.

"The plate's hot. Be careful."

She walked away before I could decide if she was being handsy.

Oanen reached out and touched his plate. With a frown, he picked up his fork and started eating.

"What's the frown for?" I asked, picking up my own fork.

He chewed slowly and nodded toward my food. I took a bite and almost groaned. It was so good. Or, maybe, I was just that hungry.

"Here," Oanen said lifting a bite from his plate toward me. "You think the eggs are good? Try the hash browns."

I swallowed and opened my mouth, more than willing to eat some of his share. And, I almost spit out the ice-cold hash browns as soon as my mouth closed around his fork. Only the light press of Oanen's foot on top of mine stopped me. I chewed quickly and swallowed.

"You're an amazing man for sharing your food."

His lips twitched, and he continued to eat his cold meal. After a moment and another press to my foot, I dug into mine.

What the hell was up with our sucky waitress? There was no way his plate was hot. She'd probably stuck the damn thing in the freezer. It would explain why it took so long to bring the food out.

I chewed and watched Oanen turn his plate to get to his eggs. Then turn it again to get to his bacon. I'd never noticed that quirk before. When he cleared that plate, he slid the pancake plate toward him while shuffling the cold plate over.

"Are you almost finished?" I asked after he had taken one bite.

I didn't play with my food. Despite the weirdness of his meal, I'd quickly decimated mine.

"Yep. No rush, though. I like watching you eat."

His gaze flicked to mine, gold flooding into the blue.

"I don't even know where your mind went just now, but keep it to yourself."

His lips twitched, and he pulled out his wallet to leave money on the table.

"Let's go, troublemaker."

"Hey, I was a complete angel this time."

I followed him out of the restaurant and got into the car. He circled around the car and got in more quickly than usual.

"In a rush?" I asked.

"Maybe." He started the car and pulled out into traffic before reaching into his pocket and handing me a folded piece of paper.

"What does it say?" he asked. He tapped his fingers on the wheel showing his agitation.

I looked at the writing.

"It's an address. That's it. Where did this come from?"

"The waitress. It fell into my lap when I moved the cold plate."

"The waitress was watching you show the hooded man's picture," I said. "Do you think this is his address?"

"I do. She told us to be careful. It sure wasn't because of a hot plate."

"Dead body or mysterious address?" I said, mostly to myself. Looking at the body first meant less smell and clearing Nicolette faster if we could prove he died after Adira took her. Checking out the address meant finding the killer, clearing Nicolette, and getting to my great-grandma's place faster. Something I wasn't prepared for.

"Dead body," I said at the same time he said, "Mysterious address."

He glanced at me.

"You don't think we should check out the address first?" he asked.

"Nope. I don't trust the waitress. What if it's a setup,

and someone's there waiting for us? Impatient people make mistakes. Better to let them wait and get restless."

He focused on the road and was silent for a moment.

"Is that the only reason?"

"No. I also want to clear Nicolette's name for Eliana. There's no saying that finding this hooded guy without proving the body was killed while Nicolette was in Uttira will result in Nicolette's freedom. We'd need the guy to confess. And, I'm honestly not sure I'm up for pulling a confession from anyone right now."

"You're right. We'll check out the body."

This time, instead of taking off from the condo, he drove to Port Morris and found a quiet spot to park.

"How are we going to do this? The clouds are higher today."

"We're going in low and fast. The island's right there."

He pointed to the island just off shore. I could see bits of a crumbling building from where we stood, and I wondered if it was another illusion.

A rustle of clothes was the only warning I had before Oanen's pants landed on my head.

"You're weird, you know that?" I said.

"Just be grateful I don't wear underwear."

"Ew. And under no circumstances should you start," I said.

"Because you'd miss the impressive views?" he asked close to my ear.

I shivered—this one had everything to do with proximity—as he reached around me and set the rest of his clothes in my arms.

"I don't know," I hedged. "I haven't really seen anything impressive."

He chuckled low in my ear.

"Now, you're just being mean. Ready to ride me, Fury?"

A flush erupted on my face and raced all the way to my toes. Need flooded my mind only to disappear a moment later when Oanen's feathered head nudged my back.

"Yeah. Hold on. That last comment robbed me of the ability to think, and I still need to put your clothes away." I took a moment to fan my face then filled the backpack.

The ride to the island was just as fast as he'd promised. And, the icy wind on my face actually felt good, this time.

When we landed on the same roof as before, I didn't hesitate to slide off, ditch the bag, and face the door. Oanen's low, knowing chuckle kept me flushed for an extra few moments while he dressed.

"I like this," he said, turning me in his arms.

I took a quick peek down and found all his views were covered.

"Disappointed?" he asked.

"Relieved. My face feels like it's about to burst into flames."

"It's almost as attractive as when your eyes glow."

He kissed the tip of my nose then led me toward the door.

"It won't be as bad this time," he promised.

"Does that mean the other body is gone?"

"Yes."

"Who took it?"

"We have our own version of funeral homes and morticians."

"Nope. Don't say any more. I don't want to know."

We walked down a single flight of stairs and went to another apartment on the same floor as the previous day. We didn't proceed past the first door in the hall this time.

"This is the one," he said.

He opened the door and went inside. Thankfully, there wasn't any odor. I looked around the barren apartment noting that, unlike the other guy, this one hadn't collected much. But, then I noticed dents in the carpet.

"Did someone clear this place out already?" I asked.

Oanen snapped a few pictures of the dents with his phone and spent a little time studying the patterns on the floor.

"I'll ask for more information."

He moved down the hall. Like a good little shadow, I stuck close.

We found the dragon in the bedroom. The bed was neatly made beneath him, and a folded piece of paper waited on the nightstand.

*Enforcer,*

*Stop looking for him. He's doing us all a favor.*

*Magroal*

I looked at the smiling dragon's face, trying to reconcile him with the bitter dragon I'd met the day before.

"He's the one who ate the burger and left. Call the Council. With my eyewitness sighting of this guy after Nicolette was taken plus his note, they have to let Nicolette go."

Oanen nodded but continued his examination of the guy and the room. While I waited, I sent a text to Eliana.

*Freedom is one phone call away. Get ready to say goodbye to mommy-dearest!*

I waited for a reply, but none came. A ball of worry formed in my stomach. This was the girl who rushed out of class to answer my phone call.

*Everything okay?* I texted after three minutes went by.

*Everything is fine. See you soon, hopefully.*

Relieved, I tucked my phone away and went to stare out the window. Nicolette would be cleared today, and I still didn't have a plan. But, it didn't really matter. While I could already predict what Oanen's reaction would be, the final decision about what to do was up to me. And there was no way I was going to kill someone else just so I could live.

"That was a big sigh. Ready to go?" Oanen asked.

"Yeah. Did you call the Council?"

"Not yet. I was going to wait until we were back in the car."

There was no playful striptease on the roof, which made for a colder ride back to Port Morris.

Before we even landed, I felt a strand of wicked calling to me. It grew stronger with each beat of Oanen's massive wings. I braced myself for the pull.

As soon as Oanen landed, I slipped from his back and raced for the car. At the last minute, I tossed the backpack on the ground then slammed the door shut. Closing my eyes, I tried to focus.

"Hold it in. Just don't let go," I mumbled to myself.

The intensity of the wickedness crawled under my skin. It begged for my attention. It demanded my intervention.

"You can do this. You can hold it."

The car door creaked. My eyes popped open, and I stared at Oanen. The orange glow on his face said it all.

"Is everything all right?" he asked calmly, his face a careful blank mask.

"No, I have to go to the bathroom. Get in so we can go."

He cocked his head at me as he slowly got in.

"You just lied to me."

"Stupid lie detector. Just hurry up, Oanen. We have to go."

He started the car and turned around. I refused to look at the man who was slowly walking down the side-street towards us.

"I'm trying to be patient," Oanen said quietly. "I'm trying to be understanding. But, it's hard to do when you won't tell me what's going on. Or worse. When you lie to me."

The more distance we placed between the man walking down the road and the car, the easier it was to think clearly. It didn't mean I was out of danger. I could now feel the wisps of wicked crawling under my skin. How much longer did I have before I wouldn't be able to resist it?

"Talk to me, Megan. Now." The complete authority in Oanen's voice made my fury stir.

"This is one of those times that you don't want to push, Oanen."

"This is one of those times I think I need to push."

I partially growled and groaned.

"Fine. I wanted to whip out my fury card on that guy walking down the street, okay? Given our current goals, I didn't think it was the right time to stop and punish someone. Better?"

In response, the steering wheel groaned under his white knuckled grip.

His fear hit me hard, and I mentally staggered under the weight of it.

"No. There's more you're not telling me."

"Tonight, Oanen. Whether we find anything at this address or not, we'll talk. I promise. Will you just give me until then so we can focus on helping Eliana and stopping this killer without distraction?"

"The distraction is there, Megan, whether we talk about it or not. But, yes. I'll drop it for now, and we'll talk tonight."

He turned his golden gaze on me.

"No exceptions. No more delays."

We parked across the street from a house that looked exceptionally normal. The well-kept, three-story home was squished between two not so nice-looking houses. Those houses matched the rest of the neighborhood, which was why a tingle kept worming around under my skin. I itched to get out of the car and confront the sources. But, I knew better than to give in. Instead, I tried to focus on Oanen's half of the conversation with the Council.

"Megan spoke to him the day after Nicolette was taken into custody. It proves she's not responsible."

A long drawn out pause followed that statement. I tried to read Oanen's expression for clues, but he wasn't giving much away. Not since my promise to talk after we were done here.

"I disagree," he said, "and can confidently speak on Megan's behalf that she disagrees, too."

I frowned. I trusted Oanen. He knew me well enough to speak on my behalf if he thought it necessary. Why was it necessary, though? The evidence couldn't be any clearer.

"No. Nothing has changed. She seems more tired and not as quick to anger."

"She's sitting right next to you, too," I said, "and feeling plenty of anger. What's going on?"

"I understand," he said, just before hanging up.

Without me needing to threaten bodily harm, he turned toward me and started talking.

"They don't believe Nicolette is innocent and won't remove her house arrest."

"What? Are they deaf or blind? Or just stupid?" I clenched my fists and wished I was in Uttira.

"Neither. They believe she's working with someone or maybe several people. Adira wouldn't give me more information than that. She asked how you were doing and if you've run into any wicked."

That just pissed me off more. She knew something. I was sure of it.

"Fine. Adira and the Council are once again useless. No offense to your parents."

"None taken. I agree with you. They're up to something. We'll need to prove without a doubt that Nicolette is innocent by finding the real killer."

He looked at the house, again.

"I think it's time to say hello," I said, reaching for the door.

Sleeping in until noon meant that we hadn't had much daylight when we started out. After going to the island then heading to New Jersey, not much remained. As we let ourselves in the gate, a hint of twilight creeped into the sky.

"I want you to stay behind me," Oanen said softly, holding the gate so I could pass.

"Fine." I knew he was trying to watch out for me. But no matter where I stood, if the hooded guy was truly wicked, I wouldn't be able to hold myself back. Even if Oanen was in the way.

I followed him up the steps and waited on the small porch as he knocked.

A curtain to our right moved a few moments prior to the door opening. Instead of the guy from the bar, a young woman looked at us questioningly.

"Can I help you?"

"I hope so," Oanen said. "We're looking for someone." He pulled out his phone and showed her the picture of the hooded man.

I saw the flicker of recognition in her eyes before she looked up at us.

"Sorry. I can't help you."

"Can't or won't?" I asked.

"My name is Oanen Quill. This is Megan Smith. We're here on behalf of the Uttira Council," he said. "And, you know what that is because you knew not to lie just now. How do you know this man?"

She started to shut the door.

Oanen stepped forward to block it with his hand. As soon as his palm crossed the plane of the threshold, he flew backward. He hit the fence with a metal clatter and crashed to the ground.

Rage filled me, and I turned to the door.

"Elizabeth Sias, open the damn door."

"Megan, quiet," Oanen said. The strain in his words made my anger worse.

I fisted my hand, ready to beat down the puny panel

keeping me from kicking the ass of the girl who just fried my boyfriend.

Oanen's fingers captured mine.

"I'm fine. And you just figured out her name," he said softly. "And, right now, she's talking on the phone. I'm trying to listen."

His explanation and a quick glance at him calmed some of my anger.

"It'll take more than a fence to hurt me. You know that." He kissed my temple gently then slowly tugged me away from the door.

"We're looking for a man named Zayn. Elizabeth knows him well. She told him not to come home."

"So a girlfriend, wife, or relative."

"Exactly what I'm thinking. And if that's the case, he's on his way here because he'll want to keep her safe."

"She's not in danger."

"He doesn't know that. And right now, she's watching us leave. When the car doesn't move, she'll let him know."

We got back into the car. Street lights came on, and the curtain in the window moved again.

"Stay here. No matter what," he said reaching for his door.

"Where are you going?"

"To the roof. I'll be able to see more from up there." He paused and gave me a stern look. "Say it. Say you'll keep your butt in that seat no matter what."

My fury stirred again, and I couldn't keep my mouth shut.

"No. What you really want me to say is that you're cute

when you're all domineering. Not going to happen, bird boy. Bossy isn't attractive."

His pupils dilated noticeably.

"Megan…"

"I will stay in the car. Now, stop being a bully and go fly away."

He exhaled slowly and left the car without kissing me, an indication of how far I'd pushed him.

Sulking, I watched the house.

What the hell was my problem? Everything was off. My temperature. My mood. My ability to sense any wickedness. My ability to send the wicked to hell. I was a broken fury. And if I wasn't careful, I was going to break one of the few things I still had going right.

Restless and feeling sorry for myself, I pulled out my phone and called Eliana.

"Yeah, what's up?" she answered, sounding annoyed.

"Everything okay?"

"Get off my pillow. I told you not to do that," she said in a strained and slightly muffled voice. Before I could ask what she was talking about, her words became clear again. "I need to find Piepen a better home."

A high-pitched squeal came from the background followed by fervent begging.

"You do what you need to do," I said, feeling bad I'd made a mess for Eliana. It seemed I was on a roll for messing up relationships.

"Thanks. I gotta go."

The line went dead.

Sighing, I pocketed the phone and leaned back in my

seat. Rather than focus on the wisps of wicked around me, I closed my eyes.

"You can do this, Megan."

"Wake."

The word echoed in my mind, pulling me from a deep sleep. If not for the ache in my shoulder and the chill penetrating my legs, I would have tried to ignore the command. Uncomfortable and more than a little cranky because of my discomfort, I opened my eyes to look for my pillow and blanket.

Instead of seeing familiar bedroom walls, I saw a face I knew well from the picture on my phone.

"You," I said, trying to sit up. I couldn't get my hands under myself.

"Here," he said, reaching for me. "Let me help you."

He helped me from my side-lying position to sitting up against a beam.

I frowned at my bound hands and feet, confused. I couldn't remember confronting him or trying to send him to hell. Nothing new hurt on me. No burns. So then, what had happened? How was I no longer in the car, and why wasn't I angry?

Giving my bonds an experimental tug, I studied the now unhooded-man.

"Zayn, right?"

"Correct. And those are magic bindings," he said. "Like last time." He tilted his hand and studied me. "How did you get out of the last ones?"

"Why don't I want to send you to hell?"

He smiled slightly.

"Because I've been good lately, not breaking any rules. Human or non-human."

A shimmer in the air just behind him caught my attention. I sat in the center of another large space. A table lit with a dangling overhead light lay just behind the guy squatting before me. However, between him and the table, a shimmer of something moved in the air, creating a bubble around us.

"More magic?" I asked.

"Yes. For your protection. I've invited a few people here and wasn't sure if you'd be ready to face them."

"What do you mean?"

He shifted slightly on the balls of his feet, pivoting just enough to expose the three older men sitting at the table. Their rough, weathered faces were turned in our direction. Their dark eyes were filled with a weary acceptance I'd seen before.

"They are dragons with more years than either of us can hope to see. And with those years come a lot of mistakes." He shrugged lightly. "Or, rather, choices a fury might not agree with."

That last statement drew my attention back to the hooded man.

"You know what I am and took me anyway?" I asked.

"I know what you are, and I know once you understand, you'll have no reason to come after me."

"I doubt that."

"You've said it yourself. You have no desire to punish me. That's because I've done nothing wrong."

My gaze flicked back to the dragons.

"Why do I need protection from them?"

His grin widened.

"This shield isn't to protect you from them but from yourself. You're a fourth-generation fury, and I don't want you burning yourself out. The last thing I want is for the other three to come after me because I wasn't careful."

I snorted.

"Right."

"What part do you doubt? My fear of you or my care?"

"Any of it. All of it."

"I know a lot of things I shouldn't. Trust me when I say I will take the utmost care of you. Now, be patient and listen. You'll understand what's going on soon enough."

He patted my stretched-out leg and stood, leaving the shield. As soon as he stepped through it, the shimmer turned into an opaque green like I was sitting in an upside-down glass bowl. My ears popped painfully, but I could suddenly hear things. Seagulls crying out. Distant traffic. The quiet murmur of deep voices coming from the table.

I could also feel.

One of those three dragons was not like the others. Oh, they all had a level of wicked that made my skin feel too tight. But, one of them had done things that begged me to send him straight to hell. My gaze locked on the one with longer, grey-streaked hair he kept back in a low ponytail.

I opened my mouth, the words to demand a confession from Rylee McGoan on the tip of my tongue. However, not a sound emerged.

Rage clawed at my middle, and I struggled with my bonds.

"We'll need to speak quickly," Zayn Sias said. "I don't know how long that spell will hold her."

"Why is she here? Why are we here?" the dragon closest to me asked. His dark eyes watched me instead of Zayn.

"She's here as a witness. You're here because each of you has spoken to me about your desire for the old ways to return. About your discontent with the way things are now.

"I cannot change your lives for you. I cannot miraculously fulfill your dreams of flying free or eating whatever you'd like. None of us can break those rules without consequence. And that's why she's here. To be a witness. So that she knows, and so that you know, what I'm saying is the truth and what I'm doing is within the bounds of what we are allowed to do."

While he spoke, my anger and the need to free myself intensified. Knowing what would happen, when I gave into the urge gripping me hard, didn't even give me pause.

My gaze remained focused on the furthest of the three men; and the intense, burning need to punish only grew stronger with each passing second. The space within my magic cage began to warm and reflect an orange glow. And, it wasn't just from my eyes.

I could feel the fire growing inside of me. I tried to hold it back. I knew what would happen if I completely gave in to it. I could feel my old burns starting to tingle with pain. Yet, I was helpless to completely stop what was happening or my need to punish.

"Get to the point, Druid," the middle dragon growled.

"Yes, of course. I'm here to offer you an opportunity to be free of your oppression. To make a stand against it. To give your life for it. I won't promise redemption. I won't promise you will go to a better place once you're gone. But I can promise your soul will be used to create something that will always stand against those who wish to oppress the unique and undesired."

A tingle of pain encircled my wrists, and I looked down at my bonds. Green sparks flew from the metal as flames engulfed my hands. Like the last few times my fire appeared, it seared my skin. And, like the last few times, I couldn't stop any of it.

I opened my mouth to cry out, but nothing came. In agony, I raged against my silence, the rage feeding my fury to the point where I stopped feeling.

"You want to kill us?" the first dragon asked. "Use us in some type of ritual sacrifice?"

"Yes," Zayn said with not an ounce of shame or remorse.

He'd just admitted to wanting to kill them; yet, I still felt not even a hint of wickedness from him and everything from the three dragons.

"You've all admitted to me that you're weary of this existence. That you're tired of what this world has to offer you. I'm offering to help you find a quick and peaceful end. An opportunity to use what's left of your existence in a way that strikes a small blow of retribution against those who oppressed you. That's all. If you're not interested, you are free to leave. There's no spell keeping you here. If you are interested, I will willingly accept the gift of your soul, and I will respect any dying wishes that you have."

The metal binding my wrists burst apart with a loud snap. Zayn, who'd been focused on the dragons, glanced at me as I reached for the bindings on my ankles.

"We don't have much time," he said. "As soon as the fury is free, you will want to be gone."

I set my hands on my ankles and watched the flames burn through the shackles there. Free, I got to my feet and moved to the green surrounding me. It sizzled and sparked as I neared it.

All four of the men were watching me now. Zayn's eyes were filled with urgency. We both knew it wouldn't be long now.

"There's nothing else I can say that will convince you of my need," Zayn said rapidly. "Many others have already given their souls to my cause. They believed their willing sacrifice would earn them a place in whatever god's realm upon their death. I can't say I believe the same, but I swear you will live on because of your soul-sacrifice. Who among you is ready to be done with this world? Who among you is ready to commit one more act of defiance against those who oppressed you? Who among you will help me?"

I pressed both hands against the barrier. Light engulfed me to the point it was hard to see. Outside the magic bowl, the men squinted.

The dragon who had been quiet so far, the one pulling me with his wickedness, finally spoke.

"I will."

And with two words, he set my world on fire.

"He is mine!" I screamed.

Rage consumed me. Ablaze, I could feel my skin giving way to the fury. I struck the shield with my fists, raining blows on the druid's magic.

Two of the dragons fled seconds before I burned through the shield.

"No!" Zayn yelled as I stepped through the remnants of the shimmer. "Please, I need him."

Yet, he didn't try to stop me from reaching out for the dragon.

The old one stood as I stopped before him, his steady gaze on me. He didn't flinch as I reached out and grabbed him by the neck.

"Don't do this," Zayn begged. "How many burns do you have already? You can't condemn him to hell. You can only condemn yourself."

His words barely registered through the words ricocheting in my mind.

"Rylee McGoan, confess."

"Fury, I have done many things in my life. More than most. Confessing would take more time than either of us cares to give. Take me to hell. If you can." His gaze shifted to the druid who was mumbling something I couldn't understand.

"Maybe next time, Fury," the dragon said with a slight smile.

"No. This time, I'll get it right."

"Rylee McGoan, I condemn you to he—" A bone-shattering ache exploded in my core. My mouth opened in a silent scream as the flames finished engulfing me.

Darkness extinguished my vision, but not before I saw the fire spread to Rylee, who smiled serenely at me.

"Fury?"

A trickle of cold water splashed on my face. I turned my

head and opened my mouth, taking a small drink and sputtering.

"Thank the useless gods," a familiar voice said. "I thought you'd gone too far and burned yourself out."

I wasn't so sure I hadn't. My skin felt raw and exposed. Like I'd been burned all over. That thought created an avalanche of memories that dumped on me all at once.

Opening my eyes, I groaned.

"I think I can help you heal a bit if you'll allow me," Zayn said.

"Yes." I didn't care what he did. I just wanted the pain to stop. Even my eyelids hurt.

He held up a tin, twisted the top off, and dug out a finger full of salve.

"Open up and try to swallow as quickly as possible. Your gag reflex will only increase the longer it sits in your mouth."

I opened up, and he swiped the paste so far back, I almost gagged anyway.

"Swallow," he said.

I did, just as the taste hit me. The rancid tang had me gagging as an aftereffect.

"Sorry. There isn't a way to make that more pleasant tasting without ruining the spell."

He reached out and pulled back the blanket covering me. I wanted to grab it back and swear, but I couldn't move. Everything hurt.

"Why am I naked?" I rasped.

"You burned everything away."

Burned away my clothes? That hadn't happened before.

He continued to look down at me. I did, too, but had to

turn my head away from the sight of my raw flesh. How close had I come to burning myself out like Zayn said?

My gaze caught on the crisp husk of a body not far from me, and I gasped. The dragon. He'd been burnt to almost nothing. Like me, his clothes were gone. Unlike me, his corpse was blackened from head to toe. A thin bone protruded from behind him, all that remained of his wings.

I closed my eyes against my impotent anger and frustration. I didn't even know what he'd done to deserve that kind of end.

The gods had done this. They'd made me this way by giving me a power that I couldn't control and didn't understand. All the anger I felt in that moment was directed at them for robbing me of the life I should have had.

Something wet trailed from the corner of my eye.

"I don't understand," Zayn said. "The paste should be helping."

# CHAPTER THIRTEEN

THE DRUID'S CONCERN CUT THROUGH MY SELF-LOATHING. I turned my head away from what I'd done and opened my eyes. As I moved, I noticed there was less pain than before.

"The paste is helping. I don't hurt as much," I assured him.

"You're crying blood, though."

"Yeah, that's just something I do when I'm upset."

I wiped away the tears, careful of my tender skin.

"Or when you're in extreme pain," Zayn said.

I eased myself into a sitting position and tucked the edges of the blanket under my butt, a thin barrier against the cold cement.

"How do you know so much about furies?" I asked.

He gave me a wry smile.

"I'd prefer not to say. Why are you upset?"

I waved a hand at the dragon and exhaled heavily.

"I hate what I am. What I do. I don't even know what the dragon did to deserve that, but I couldn't stop it."

Zayn, who'd been hunkered down on the balls of his

feet, sat and studied me. In turn, I did the same. This was the first time I really looked at him without his hood up. And, everything I'd noted before had been done in a fog of panic or anger. I hadn't noticed the green flecks in his kind, hazel eyes or how his hair was long enough it was showing a hint of wave as it fell around his head in disarray. Mostly, I hadn't noticed the crease lines marking his forehead. A sign of constant worry or constant surprise?

"In all the research I've done," he said slowly, "I've never heard of a fury who didn't embrace what she was."

"Yeah, well, I didn't know what I was until a few months ago. My mom ditched me in Uttira without a word of explanation. I thought I was human."

"That had to be a shock."

I shrugged lightly.

"Not as much as it should have been. I guess deep down, I knew something was wrong with me."

"Wrong?"

"I don't want to be who I am. I don't know what the hell is going on half the time. I hate the urges I have to hurt people when I don't even know why. The gods are assholes for making me this way."

"Not gods. Just one. You serve Hades."

"Awesome. Know where he is? I'd like to throat punch the asshole."

Zayn laughed.

"He'd probably find it amusing. You furies are like his daughters. I'm not sure there's much you could do wrong in his eyes."

"Lovely."

"You didn't kill him, by the way. The dragon, I mean."

I arched a brow and glanced at the burnt body.

"His current condition would beg to differ," I said.

"He was gone before the flames consumed him. I gave him the peaceful, quick end he'd asked for. It wasn't murder. I had his consent."

"I'm too tired and hurt to care one way or another. As long as you're gone before I get my wicked radar back, we're good." I studied his hazel eyes for a moment. "Why are you doing this? Killing all these creatures?"

"Not killing," he said with a pacifying gesture. "I collect their life-energy, or soul, depending on whatever you believe, which they gave freely."

"Okay. But why?"

He grew serious and slightly sad.

"You saw my sister. She's a prisoner of her own home. Because of magic. Because the gods are cruel and made my twin mortal."

Twin? I wasn't expecting that.

Somewhere nearby, a phone buzzed.

"What's your name?" he asked.

"Megan Smith."

"I'm glad I met you. I hope you'll remember this conversation when you wake."

INSISTENT BUZZING near my ear brought me back out of my magically induced sleep. There was no groggy disorientation this time. I knew right where I was and exactly what had happened. It was hard not to remember with the throbbing pain drumming inside my skull and the sickening dance going on in my stomach. I opened my eyes and managed to prop myself up enough so I could throw up.

When I finished heaving, I looked around.

Zayn was gone. He'd left behind his jacket, though, which he'd laid over me for extra warmth. And my phone. He must have removed it from my coat before sticking me in his shield. I hadn't even thought to check for it after freeing my hands. I'd been too busy with the fury fire burning inside of me.

While I was grateful it hadn't burned up with the rest of my things, I was more grateful that I hadn't thrown up on it. I needed to call Oanen. He was probably worried as hell.

Sighing, I sat up and winced at the pain on my forearms. Zayn's paste had healed most of the burns I'd gained from my little stunt, but the deeper ones on both forearms remained. They throbbed in time with the older burns.

I hissed out a breath and wished I had more of Zayn's ass-paste to eat.

I frowned at that thought, knowing it hadn't come out right.

My phone buzzed again, distracting me, and I picked it up. Oanen's name showed brightly on the display.

"Hello?" I answered.

"Where are you?" His clipped, angry words made me smile. I'd never been so glad to hear his voice.

"I'm not sure. And no, I'm not going outside to check. I'm lying naked on the floor with a blanket and a jacket covering me."

Nothing but silence answered me for several, long heartbeats.

"Whose?"

"Whose what?"

"Whose jacket is covering you?"

"That doesn't matter. Just come get me. I'll turn on my GPS and text you the location."

The line went dead. That seemed a bit overdramatic. I wrinkled my nose at the phone but did as I said I would. Less than a second after I sent the location, he sent back that he was on his way.

With a sigh, I scooted away from my vomit pile and lay back down on the cold floor. It felt good on my head but was making the rest of me ache.

I dozed lightly until a door banged nearby.

"Megan?" Oanen's voice rang out.

"Here."

I didn't bother trying to sit up. I was too tired. Too cold.

Steps scraped against the floor, drawing closer.

When I blinked my eyes open, Oanen was there, already bending down toward me. His carefully blank mask never slipped, but the hold he had on what he was feeling did. Rage, something close to that of a fury's, filled my head along with a paralyzing fear.

"Please tell me you brought the car," I said softly. "I'm too cold to fly."

He made a pained sound and scooped me into his arms. Without a word, he turned on his heel and walked back the way he'd come.

I closed my eyes and leaned my head against his rapidly beating heart.

Moments came and went. Him buckling me in. The vibration of the tires on the road. The sound of cars. The feeling of being carried upstairs. The soft sheets rubbing against the raw places still remaining on my skin. Then, nothing for a while.

When I opened my eyes again, the pain in my head had been downgraded to a mild headache, and the sun had come up to light the bedroom.

I rolled from my side to my back and winced.

The bed beside me moved, and I looked up at Oanen, who was leaning against the headboard.

"How long have I been out?"

"Almost six hours."

I groaned and struggled to sit up, the jacket and blanket from Zayn hampering my movements.

"What happened, Megan? You promised not to leave the car."

His tone had me whipping my head in his direction mid-struggle.

"Are you serious right now? You know better than anyone else what I am. How little control I have over what I do. What the hell do you think happened?"

"I don't know. Where are your clothes? And who gave you this jacket?"

My fury lifted its head wearily.

"No," I said firmly. "I'm not doing this. I'm not going to get angry with you. And I'm not going to deal with your pouty possessiveness right now."

Ignoring the aches and pains, I threw off the jacket and blanket and rose naked from the bed.

"I burned away my clothes and a lot of my skin. Zayn Sias, the druid we've been looking for, covered me and gave me some paste to make the worst of it go away.

"When you're in your right mind, I'll keep my promise, and we'll talk."

I turned my back to him, ignored his soft curse, and marched my butt to the bathroom. After I used the toilet and brushed my teeth, I attempted a shower. It didn't last longer than a hurried hair wash to remove the puke smell. Instead of reaching for a towel to dry off, I just stood there, dripping.

On the other side of the iced-glass partition, the bathroom door opened.

"Did you send him to hell?" Oanen asked.

"No. I can't send anyone to hell. All I do is hurt myself every time I try."

"You hurt yourself trying to send him to hell?"

"No. He's innocent as far as my fury is concerned. I didn't do anything to him."

There was a long moment of silence.

"I'm trying to understand, Megan, but you're making it hard."

I knew he was trying to understand what had happened to me, but he was focusing on who I was with rather than what happened to me. I opened the door so he would get the full picture.

His gaze swept over me, lingering on the burn on my chest and the ones on my hip and arms.

"There's the burn on my back, too. Four times, Oanen. Since the lake, I've tried to send someone to hell four times. Each time, I pass out and wake up with a burn and the inability to feel wickedness."

Understanding started to light his eyes as he crossed his arms.

"The numbness doesn't last long. A day or two, at most. Then I start feeling the wickedness again. That's what I was feeling yesterday in the car. The wickedness was everywhere, but I was sitting there trying to resist the urge to get out and beat someone because I'd promised you I'd stay put. I don't know what happened next. I don't remember leaving, only waking up where you found me.

"Zayn was there along with three dragons. He's not what we thought he was."

"What's that?" Oanen asked softly.

"A killer. He isn't killing the people we're finding dead. He's asking them for their life-force. And some of them are so unhappy with their lives, they're willingly giving it." I looked at the burns on my arms. "These are because one of the dragons was wicked. Very, very wicked. I wanted to hurt him so badly that I couldn't stop myself." I closed my eyes and took a deep breath.

"I remember grabbing him by his throat and then feeling pain. So much pain. When I came to, the dragon was burnt to a crisp. But, Zayn was still there. He was worried I'd pushed myself too far and was trying to heal me. The paste he gave me helped take away some of the pain and heal some of the burns.

"I don't know what he's doing with the life forces he's collecting, but I don't think it's for anything bad. If it was, I would have sensed his wickedness last night before I tried punishing the dragon."

"I don't care about who's wicked or punished or any of that," Oanen said, slowly stalking toward me.

"What I care about is standing in front of me. Bruised. Battered. In pain. And I can't do a thing about it. You're killing me, Megan. Slowly. Methodically. And I can't walk away."

He stopped in front of me and gently put his forehead against mine. I felt every ounce of his anguish.

"I'm sorry," I whispered, hurting for both of us.

"Those aren't the words I want to hear."

I knew what words he wanted. And even though admitting it terrified me, I owed him the truth.

"I love you, Oanen. So much it hurts to breathe at the thought you might be ready to give up on me."

His hand cupped the back of my head.

"Never," he said just before his lips touched mine.

He stole my breath with each gentle taste and touch until I broke away, panting. He set his forehead on mine again.

"Thank you," he said softly.

"I didn't do anything."

"You did. You gave me your heart. It's mine. Now and always. It's all I've wanted since our first flight."

I smiled softly before reality intruded.

"We need to call the Council and tell them what happened."

He exhaled heavily and pulled back from me.

"I doubt they'll listen. They know there's something wrong with your abilities and aren't trusting your word."

My fury tried to lift her head again.

"Nope," I said firmly. "Not worth it. Save your strength."

Oanen gave me an odd look.

"I'm not going to let my fury get riled up over the Council. She needs a break, or my powers will kill me."

His expression grew serious, and as he moved away to grab some ointment, I continued to air dry and stare off into space.

"We can't sit here and do nothing. We know what Nicolette is like. How she gets in a person's head and makes them do things they might not want to do otherwise. If she does that to Eliana…"

"Eliana is stronger than you think," he said.

"She's also more fragile than you want to admit."

Oanen started spreading ointment on my burns, soothing the rest of my pain. It was nice having someone wait on me.

My eyes widened.

"Elbner," I said loud enough to make Oanen wince.

"Sorry. I just realized we have a witness. Elbner can tell the Council it was Zayn."

"Elbner is still spelled."

"Yes, but once it's out that we know it's Zayn, it's common knowledge; and he'll be able to speak it. Just like the library, right?"

Oanen's lips twitched.

"I love seeing the excitement in your eyes," he said.

"I gotta get my phone."

I moved to run from the bathroom at the same moment he reached forward to dab more salve on my front. Instead of touching the burn, his fingers brushed the top of my right breast. We both froze.

Gold exploded in his eyes, and his palm slowly closed over me, making my skin tingle with an expanding warmth.

"Please don't take this the wrong way," I said breathlessly, "but this really isn't the right time."

He nodded, but his fingers began stroking the sensitive skin. I pressed forward into his palm. His hand lightly tested the weight and shape of me. Then his thumb brushed over the peak.

I struggled to keep my head as heat licked its way from my middle upward. Need scorched me, and I knew it wasn't all my own when his pupils dilated.

"Oanen. We need to think of Eliana."

He made a pained noise and removed his hand.

"Go."

I fled the bathroom and grabbed my phone from the nightstand. It was hard to hear the dial tone over the beating of my heart.

"Eliana, you need to get to Elbner," I said as soon as she answered. "Tell him I know his master was Zayn Sias. I know Zayn was the one responsible for all the creatures who died with a smile. Tell Elbner I'm making it common knowledge. Once you do that, you should be able to take him to the Council as a witness. Got it?"

"Yes. Zayn Sias. Got it. Thank you."

She hung up without saying anything else. I could only imagine how stressed out she was with her mom there.

A gentle touch to my back had me looking over my shoulder. Oanen's gaze was locked on the burn there, but I could tell from his eyes that his mind was still focused on something else.

"I don't think there's anything else for us to do here," I said.

"Oh, I think there's plenty to do."

"I mean, now that we know the cause behind the deaths, we should probably leave. Track down my great-grandma." Even as I said it, I mentally cringed at the idea.

"There's no rush. We can wait a few days for you to heal."

I knew what he had in mind while we waited and turned fully to capture his hands.

"I don't think you understand."

"I'll admit it's been a little hard to focus with you walking around naked."

"You do it all the time."

He nodded slowly, letting his gaze drift downward, and sighed wistfully.

"But I don't look like you."

I snorted a laugh.

"Don't move."

He stayed where I left him while I went to his suitcase and grabbed one of his button-down shirts. It was soft and big and easier to put on than a t-shirt. With the sleeves rolled up and only a few middle buttons used, it didn't bother any of my burns, either.

He groaned as I walked toward him.

"You have no idea how sexy you are. Wearing my shirt just made it so much better."

"Focus, Oanen."

He heaved a sigh and sat on the edge of the bed.

"What don't I understand?"

"I'm stuck in a spiral of self-destruction. I feel someone wicked, try to send them to hell, burn myself in the process, and suppress my abilities for a few days just to do it all again. Only I'm not healing. Or regulating my temperature like I used to. I'm more tired every time."

The concern on his face grew the longer I spoke.

"What are you saying?"

"When I woke up on the floor with Zayn hovering over me, he said, 'I thought you burned yourself out.' And he's not the first one to say something like that."

I sat beside Oanen and took his hand in mine, already knowing how angry he was going to be.

"Stop saying his name," Oanen said. "I'm trying not to think about how he took you from right under my nose. I want to kill him for that."

"He didn't do anything bad."

"How can you say that? You said he put you to sleep."

"So has Adira."

"Exactly. I think it's safe to say you hate her."

"Different reasons. Adira is a pain in my ass and doesn't share information. It's hard to hate a guy who gives up his coat and doesn't cop a peek. At least, I don't think he did."

Oanen's expression hardened.

"You're not helping," he said.

"And you're keeping us off topic."

"Right. Just stop saying his name, and we'll be fine."

"As I was saying, the hooded-guy—"

"That's not any better."

"—isn't the only one to say I'll burn myself out. I didn't tell you everything my mom said that day in the diner."

Oanen waited for me to continue.

"Her exact words were, 'You can't deliver the wicked to hell without your wings because without your wings, you're not a fury, and your power will consume you.'"

His fingers twitched around mine.

"Why didn't you tell me?"

"I knew what you'd want me to do. And I can't, Oanen. If I kill my great-grandma just to claim my power, won't I become one of the wicked I'm here to punish? I can't kill her just so I can live. There has to be another way."

He said nothing, just looked down at our joined hands, his thumb slowly stroking the skin on the back of mine.

"What do you want to do?" he asked finally.

"I don't know. I didn't tell you all of this sooner because I thought I'd come up with something better than just going to St. Louis to talk to my grandma and seeing if she has any answers."

"Why isn't that an option?"

"It is an option. I'm just worried that when we get there, she won't have answers or won't give them. Then, you'll want me to do what my mom wants just to keep me from getting hurt more than I already am."

He nodded slowly, and when he looked up at me, his eyes were blue again.

"You're right. That's what I'd want because I'm selfish and desperate to keep you with me. But, if the last twenty-four hours has taught us anything, it's that I can't force you to do something you don't want to do. Or stop you from doing something that's in your nature to do. I don't want to change you, Megan. I want to love you just as you are."

I leaned over and set my head against his shoulder.

"Ditto, bird boy. I'm sorry I came down so hard on you for being jealous. If the roles were reversed, I probably would have acted the same."

"The difference is that I love it when you get jealous over me."

I grinned and nudged him.

"You're insane to provoke my fury like that. I don't think she'll share well once we're officially…"

"Mated?"

My face flushed.

"Yeah. That."

His phone rang, saving me from any further embarrassment.

"Hello?" He listened quietly for a minute. "No. You're going to need to send someone else for him. Megan needs to get to St. Louis. Her powers are killing her. And, I'll blame you if that happens."

He hung up and looked at me.

"Please tell me that wasn't your mom," I said.

# CHAPTER FOURTEEN

Oanen's lips twitched, and he reached out to toy with the ends of my hair.

"No, that wasn't my mom. It was Adira."

"Oh, I bet being told 'No' made her real happy. Should we expect a portal?"

He shook his head.

"I doubt it. She won't admit this, but she's afraid of you. They all are."

"Good."

I rubbed my head and wished I could just take a nap.

"Are you hungry?" he asked.

"No. But I should eat."

While Oanen went to order food for us, I dug out the *Book of Fury* to read again. Gaining the little bit of understanding I had didn't help me grasp any more information from the book. However, the parts that talked about the power consuming me now made more sense.

Oanen finally brought me a burger and fries, which I nibbled on while reclined in bed. I must have dozed off because when I next woke, he was in bed with me, and we were both lying flat. As soon as I shifted to a more comfortable position, he opened his eyes and looked at me.

"Sorry. The spot on my back was hurting."

"It's okay. Just making sure you're not going anywhere."

"No. I think it'll be a day or two before I feel any wickedness again." I moved a little closer to him and rested my head on his shoulder.

He stroked my back, careful to avoid the raw patch.

"Good, but I still don't think I'll sleep very deeply tonight. Just in case."

I didn't have the same problem. I slept hard and woke grudgingly just before dawn when my bladder refused to be ignored any longer.

"Going to the bathroom," I whispered softly as I eased away from Oanen.

He made a sound of affirmation and rolled to his side, his breathing still soft and even. I wondered how long he'd stayed awake to keep an eye on me. It must have been a while because he was still in the same position when I returned.

Easing into bed so as not to disturb him, I settled next to him. His warmth soothed me, and I exhaled contentedly. However, I'd slept so much that I couldn't fall back to sleep. So I lay there thinking.

Why was it so easy for me to know what everyone else wanted me to do and so hard for me to know what I wanted? I knew exactly what I did not want to do. But what did I want?

I decided what I really wanted was to go about my life my own way and not the way the gods wanted me to go.

That didn't mean I was unwilling to have a task or job. To be useful in some way. When I really thought about it, I liked the idea of being part of something bigger than myself. I just didn't want to feel cornered or manipulated into doing something I didn't want to do.

I mean, why make some of us crave flesh and then condemn us to hell for answering the craving? Was everything just a test to see how we exercised our free will? What about those impulses some of us couldn't control? I couldn't fight the way rage consumed me whenever anyone wicked was around. What was the point of my existence, then? Was I truly only here to hurt others?

My thoughts went round and round until the sun rose, and Oanen jerked awake. I smiled when he rolled over, searching for me.

"Morning," I said.

He exhaled when he saw I was where he'd left me, and I smiled wider.

"Worried you'd lost something, again?"

"You have no idea. How long have you been awake?"

I shrugged and tilted my head to look at the clock.

"Almost two hours, I think."

He gently tucked me close to him again, and his lips brushed over the column of my throat. My eyes rolled back in my head at the sensation.

"Mmm." I couldn't help the sound. Every time he touched me, it just got better.

He groaned and pressed another kiss to my skin before getting out of bed.

"Don't make sounds like that, Megan. I don't have the restraint."

I watched him walk to the bathroom, glad he couldn't see my stupid grin. I liked that I was his weakness.

While he showered, I went to the kitchen and poured myself a bowl of cereal. He reemerged with shorts riding low on his waist and tousled wet hair before I finished my breakfast. In that glance, I knew he was my weakness, too.

"So what time do you want to leave?" I asked.

"I don't know yet. It's up to you."

"What do you mean?" I asked. I didn't miss the way his gaze skimmed my exposed legs as I sat there in his shirt.

"You're the one who has to face your great-grandmother, and you're right that she might have a better answer than what your mom already gave you. I'm not going to push you to leave until you're ready."

"But what about when I start feeling things again?"

"This place is warded. Unlike the druid's house, the warding here will keep out sound and emotion. You're safe here for as long as you need."

"And as soon as I step outside, the collective wickedness of this city will bring me to my knees. It's better if we leave before I get my powers back. We don't have to go to St. Louis. We can go anywhere. Somewhere quiet." I realized the flaw in my thinking as soon as I said it. If I waited to go to St. Louis, I'd run into the same problem I was trying to avoid when leaving New York.

"Crap," I said under my breath.

"Why don't you try your mom again?" he suggested.

I snorted. "What for?"

"You know more now. You understand what she's talking about. Maybe this time you'll be able to get through to her about why you don't want to kill your great-grandma."

I sighed heavily. "Normal humans would never have this conversation. No one kills grandmas."

"I don't know. The humans made a Christmas song about it."

"That doesn't count. It was Santa."

I froze and looked at Oanen in wide-eyed shock.

"Is Santa real?"

Oanen threw his head back and laughed. The sound did things to my middle and made me wish I wasn't hurt.

He turned away, still chuckling.

"I'll get your phone," he said.

I finished eating and put my bowl in the sink before he returned. This time, he also had a pair of shorts for me to put on.

Smiling, I accepted the phone and set the shorts aside. I sat down again and crossed my legs to expose one thigh up to my hip. Gold started to appear in his gaze.

Letting that distract me, I dialed my mom's number.

"This better not be another call from New York," Mom answered.

"We need to meet and talk in person again."

"Why? Everything you need to know is in the book."

"Obviously it's not, or I wouldn't have four very large burns on my body. Two of them I blame on you."

"The note said to get your ass to St. Louis to kill your Grandma Irene. I gave a name and address. That's everything you needed, Megan. Now get your ass into your lover boy's car and get to your grandma."

Frustration clawed at me because I knew that even if my

mom would shut up and listen for two seconds, she still wouldn't give a damn about how I felt about all of this.

"How does a mom just stop loving her only child? I hope I never have kids."

Without waiting for her reply, I hung up.

Oanen caught the phone when I threw it.

"Don't let your mom's poor parenting skills close the door on having your own kids," he said softly.

I cringed, realizing what I'd said.

The phone in his hand started ringing, and he looked down at it.

"It's your mom."

I shook my head. "No. It's Paxton. And I don't need to talk to her."

Instead of setting the phone down, he answered and put the call on speakerphone.

"Megan's listening," he said.

"I never stopped loving you, Megan," my mom said in a much calmer tone. "I'm telling you to get to your grandma to save you. You set your power free, but without wings, you can't use it. It'll burn you up. You need to get to your grandma."

"No. I'm not going to kill her just to save myself. It doesn't make sense. We punish the wicked. How is killing her not going to be wicked?"

"It will be. But it doesn't matter. That's how we're made. You have to kill her, Megan."

"Never."

The call went dead. I made a face and looked up at Oanen.

"I hate to say this, but I told you so. She's useless." I

thrummed my fingers on the counter, trying to think of what I wanted to do next.

"The smartest move would be to get out of New York now," I said, mostly to myself. Then inspiration struck.

"My mom isn't the only one who knows things." I glanced at Oanen. "The guy who shall not be named also knows stuff. Maybe he knows something—"

"Stop right there. We are not tracking him down so you can ask him for advice. You seem to be forgetting that he stole you."

"He borrowed me to clear his name. And, he returned me unharmed."

"He didn't return you. He left you broken and burned in a pool of your own vomit."

"That pool wasn't there when he left."

"I don't care."

I huffed an aggravated sigh.

"Between your jealousy and my fear of killing my grandma, which one wins?" I asked.

Oanen's expression cracked.

"Fine. We'll check out his house tomorrow."

"Tomorrow? What's wrong with today?"

"I barely survived yesterday," Oanen said. "Give me some time to recover. I just want to keep you here where it's safe. Twenty-four hours of just us. That's all I'm asking."

"Okay, but you better be ready to entertain me. I don't do bored."

Gold crept back into his gaze.

"I'm sure I can think of something fun to do."

I WOKE with a stretch and a smile. True to his word, Oanen had kept me very entertained the day before. Coed showering was now my new favorite sport. He'd been careful not to touch anything that would hurt, which meant we hadn't done a whole heck of a lot. But what we had managed had been amazing.

When we ran out of warm water, there had been movies to entertain us. And lots of couch snuggling. I was glad he'd asked for twenty-four hours. We'd needed it.

I looked at the clock, saw it wasn't yet 6 a.m., and rolled over with a smile, ready to tell him he still had two hours left. My smile faded when I saw his spot was empty. I stretched out a hand and felt the sheets were already cold.

Getting out of bed, I went in search of him. However, the condo was empty except for me and a box of cereal that had been set out on the counter along with my phone. I picked up my phone and saw a message from Oanen and another from Eliana. I read Oanen's first.

*I brought the phone out here so it wouldn't wake you. Went to find Zayn. I'll call when I have him, so you can talk to him on the phone. Stay in the condo.*

I smiled slightly and debated whether or not to call him out on forgetting our whole sticking together promise. I decided it wasn't worth it. I knew his reasons for leaving me behind. The condo was the safest place for me because of the spell to keep stuff out. Staying here also kept me a healthy distance away from the guy who stole me. This time, my grin widened at Oanen's jealousy. I'd never admit it, but it was cute when it made him protective. Just not when he got overbearing with it.

I opened the other message from Eliana.

*My mom is free but not leaving.*

Swearing softly, I dialed Eliana's number. She picked up right away, despite the time. But, that didn't necessarily mean anything. I wasn't even sure what day of the week it was anymore.

"What do you mean she's not leaving?" I asked. "Does she have a choice?"

"Apparently she does now," Eliana said.

"What does that mean?"

"Adira thinks she is seeing a positive change in me with my mom being present. She also thinks I look healthier. I don't look healthier; I look angrier. The Council obviously can't tell the difference. I think they're confusing me with you."

I laughed softly.

"Give them hell, then," I said.

"Oh, I plan to."

"So, other than your mom staying, how are things back home?"

"Not too bad. I found some brownies who were willing to take Piepen in. He was a little upset by it, but I think he's adjusting well. I'm planning on visiting him later today. And, Elbner is making great progress on your house. For being such a grumpy, unkempt thing, he sure has that place looking nice. He's even started scraping the loose paint off the outside.

"Wow. I'm impressed," I said. "He knows that it's winter, though, right?"

"It doesn't seem to bother him."

"Other than that, anything new?" I was dying to blatantly ask about Fenris but didn't want to tip my hand if she wasn't aware yet.

"Nothing worth talking about," she said quickly.

I smiled into the phone. If she wasn't ready to admit it, that was fine.

"How about you?" she asked. "Is it true that a druid was involved in the deaths?"

"Yes. That would be Zayn. He's not wicked, though. That much I could sense."

"Be careful around him, Megan. It's not safe to trust druids."

"It's not safe to trust most of us," I said.

"Isn't that the truth."

After we hung up, I poured myself a bowl of cereal and turned on the TV. I managed to waste an hour that way then went to take a shower. Getting clean just wasn't the same without Oanen's help. When I was done, I went back to the phone and checked for new messages. Nothing.

Deciding to be the needy girlfriend, I started a message to Oanen.

"Did you get lost with a GPS? Come and get me. We'll look for Zayn together."

I set the phone down and went back to try to find something on TV. Every few minutes, I would glance at my phone. It never buzzed, though.

Close to noon, I finally got a text. Only it wasn't from Oanen; it was from my mom.

*Meet me at the Gizzard in 20.*

I groaned. Oanen had the car. That meant walking the streets of New York. Although it wasn't that far, if I felt anything, I'd be screwed. However, now that Mom was finally willing to meet me, I didn't want to text back asking to reschedule.

After writing a quick note and putting it on the counter, I slipped my coat and boots on and left the condo. Thankfully, when I stepped out on the street, I didn't feel a thing. I was still blissfully numb from the last burn.

Keeping my hands in my pocket and my steps quick, I made it to the Gizzard in the allotted time. A tingle of magic rippled over my skin as I open the door to a quiet and empty interior. I frowned and checked my phone. It was exactly twenty minutes since Mom's message. I looked around, again, wondering where the hell she was.

The door that led to the back hall opened, and Mom stepped out. She looked me over and crossed her arms.

"Good. You're here. Now, you're going to listen."

"Me? I should have known you weren't ready to actually help."

I turned to leave.

"Oanen's been gone a long time, hasn't he?" she asked, stopping me cold. "When was the last time you heard from him?"

I turned slowly, a sinking ball of fear and fury forming in my stomach.

"What did you do?"

"Nothing a loving mother wouldn't do." She tossed me a phone, which I caught by reflex. "I gave you motivation, Megan."

I looked at the phone's screen and saw Oanen's red face glaring back at me.

"What did you do?" I repeated, my voice deadly calm.

Through the haze of my anger, I noted four small ovals

on his jawline that looked redder than the rest.

"Did you burn him?"

"It was an unintentional side effect of taking him to your great-grandma's. Having the two of us that close together resulted in—"

I flew at my mother with a strangled cry, blind to reason or caution. With the back of her hand, she sent me flying across the room.

"Calm down. The picture is proof that he's alive and well enough."

I rolled to my feet and plucked a splinter of wood the size of a pencil from my bicep. It snagged on my jacket on the way out, but I barely noticed that or the blood that immediately started to trickle down my arm.

Focused on my mom, I stalked forward. Unlike the last time, I didn't rush her.

"Fighting me will resolve nothing," she said, watching me.

"No, but making you bleed will make me feel a hell of a lot better."

Mom's eyes flared bright orange as I drew closer.

"Megan Smith," she said in her fury voice.

I embraced my fury, or what was left of her, and moved fast enough to punch my mom square in the face. Her head barely moved.

"Paxton Smith," I said in my own fury voice. "Go screw yourself."

Her eyes grew brighter, and the heat of her anger started to melt the shell of my jacket. The wood floor beneath our feet crackled and blackened.

Scary fast, she reached out and gripped me by my

throat.

"I will not lose you to your own stupidity. Get your ass to St. Louis, now, and save your boyfriend."

She pushed me hard, and I went flying backward again. Barely a second after I landed, I was back up on my feet, glaring in her direction. Smoke drifted in the air between us, a murky blue haze that would have made it hard to see if fire wasn't slowly consuming my mom.

As I watched, wings sprouted from her back, vibrant twin infernos that folded forward to wrap around her torso in a bold display of yellow and orange. I knew what I was seeing. Her true form. My future true form, clothed in the fires of hell.

Zayn's comment about us being like daughters to Hades seemed more likely, looking at Mom just then.

The fire wings covering her grew impossibly bright then winked out of existence, taking her with them.

I coughed out some smoke and looked down at the phone still in my hand. The screen had cracked during one of my falls. The fissure didn't stop me from seeing Oanen's beautiful, angry face. Or his burns. Rage poked at me again as I noticed how his shoulders seemed stretched back. The image didn't show why, but I knew she'd bound his arms behind him.

First, Mom took him then tied him to a tree. Now, she wanted me to go save him. Or what? I considered the implied consequence. My family was insane. Insane enough to kill the man who held my heart? Absolutely.

The floor beneath my feet started to smolder.

"Save my boyfriend?" I said softly. "They have no idea what they've unleashed."

# CHAPTER FIFTEEN

In the smoke-filled room of the Gizzard, my mind raced. Oanen had taken his car to find Zayn. How exactly was I supposed to get to St. Louis? It was a one-day trip if I had a car and could drive straight through without stopping. A bus would be twice that. And the way I was feeling, I'd hurt someone before the bus arrived there. I needed a car.

I could try calling the Council. Or maybe, Oanen's mom. However, I doubted she'd appreciate that all the secrecy and withheld information had resulted in her son being kidnapped. And, given that my mom and grandma were involved and the Council feared me, I also doubted they would involve themselves in our family squabble.

Ignoring the burning pain in my arm, the smoke that followed me each step toward the door, and my throbbing headache, I left the Gizzard. The cold winter wind tore the accumulating heat from around me and cleared my mind long enough for me to think of another option.

I knew someone else who might help me. Maybe.

I used a ride app on my phone to get a lift to Elizabeth Sias's address.

The house looked the same—complete with moving curtain to the right as I approached. I pounded on the door, not pretending this time.

"Elizabeth," I called. "I need his help."

The door jerked open, and Zayn's sister stared at me.

"He's not here."

I swore.

"Do you have a car?"

Her glaze flicked over my jacket.

"Do you know you're smoldering and a little bloody?"

"Do you have a car and a change of clothes?" I amended.

She hesitated for a moment.

"Please, Elizabeth. I'm not after Zayn. I spoke on his behalf. What's going on with me now has nothing to do with any of that. The guy I was with? Someone took him. And I have to get him back."

"Fine. Wait right here." She moved to turn away then looked at me again. "Don't try to come in."

"I remember what happens. I'll wait here."

I watched her disappear into the depths of the house and idly wondered if the magic barrier was keeping the heat in, because I wasn't feeling anything. I waited and ignored the occasional slow car that drove by.

Elizabeth returned several minutes later with a bag along with a set of keys. The bag she tossed to me. Then, she pressed the button on the fob, and a nice-looking car almost a block away beeped.

"I hope you can replace it if you wreck it," she said.

"I can't, but I know people I can make do it. So, you're covered."

She smiled slightly.

"Good luck, Megan. Zayn said you were pretty cool."

I nodded and left, heading for the car. When I reached it, I looked into the bag. Elizabeth and I weren't close to the same size. She had a lot more height on me. While the pants wouldn't work, the shirt and jacket would. I stripped down to my bra right there on the street. Someone catcalled.

"Do it again so I can rip your tongue out and watch you eat it," I said without turning.

No one else watching made a noise. But, I could feel them. I shouldn't have been able to. Not yet. At least, I didn't think I should have this soon.

Ignoring the urge to follow through on my threat, I ripped the whole sleeve off my old shirt and used it as a bandage before putting on the new top and jacket. As far as anyone driving past me would see, I looked completely respectable and not like someone who had almost started a building on fire.

I threw the bag and my dirty clothes in the back and got into the new sedan. I didn't know what druids did exactly, but Zayn seemed to be doing well for himself. Or maybe his sister was a kickass president of some company.

"Nope," I said starting the car. "Prisoner of her own home. Doubt that works well on a resume."

I punched in granny-dearest's address and pulled away from the curb as the map app found me the fastest route.

The dash clock said it was almost two. The map app said I'd arrive tomorrow just before sunrise. I gritted my teeth and pressed the gas pedal until I was going the mandatory five over and hoped that I wouldn't run into any trouble.

Eight hours and one fueling later, I reconsidered my definition of trouble as I downed a gas station espresso and an energy drink. My eyeballs felt like they were wrapped with sandpaper, which grew grittier the longer I tried keeping them open.

"This better work," I said tossing the empty can and cup to the passenger floor.

As tired as I was, I didn't want to stop for even a few hours of sleep. I could feel the annoyance growing under my skin and feared what delaying even a few more hours would do to me when I entered St. Louis.

However, twenty-five minutes later, I was pulled over to the shoulder, peeing in a ditch and still tired as hell. Only, in addition to all that, I couldn't stop shaking.

"Stupid caffeine. Stupid fury burnout."

I pulled up my pants and got back into the car just as my phone started to ring. It wasn't a number I recognized. In the past, that meant nothing but trouble, and my anger over what potential bullshit my mom or the Council was going to throw at me next had me burning through the caffeine as I answered.

"Hello."

"Megan? This is Elizabeth. Zayn gave me your number and told me to call. Can you pull over?"

I looked around at the dark stretch of road.

"I already am."

"Great. Just a minute." Her voice became muffled. "She's pulled over."

A bright, blinding light filled the car.

"What the hell?" I dropped my phone to rub my stinging eyes.

"Sorry, Megan," Zayn said from beside me. "I haven't mastered portals without the light flare, yet."

I blinked several times until I could see him.

"I didn't know druids could do portals."

"Most can't. I'm sorry it took me so long to join you. I had some things that needed my attention before I could break away for a few hours to help you."

"Help me?"

"Elizabeth said you needed my help." He reached down and picked up my phone. "I have her. Thank you." He hung up and handed it back to me.

"If you would be so kind, I'd prefer you delete that number."

I rubbed my face tiredly, trying to stay focused on what he was saying.

"I just needed a car," I said, "not you, personally."

"To get Oanen back from your great-grandmother. I know."

"Then why are you here? And, how do you know about Oanen?"

He tapped his ear.

"I listen to the whispers. And I'm here because I think you need more than just a car. You're exhausted. Now, let's do a fire drill so I can drive for a while."

I willingly switched places with him, figuring I had a better chance of reaching my destination uninjured and faster if I did so.

"Oanen left to look for you," I said, when Zayn pulled out onto the road.

"I know. Elizabeth told me. I wasn't home at the time."

I leaned my head against the seat and watched Zayn drive. He was handsome enough, but there was something about him that said stay away. I wondered if he was close to anyone outside of his sister.

"You don't seem to be home very much," I said conversationally. "Girlfriend? Boyfriend?"

He chuckled.

"Unattached and unavailable," he said confirming my thoughts. "And, no, I'm not home often. I work a lot, and that's why I worry about Elizabeth. So why was Oanen looking for me?"

"What? Something you don't know?"

He flashed a grin at me.

"It's been known to happen on occasion."

"He was looking for you because of me. You seemed to know a lot about what I'm going through. Fourth generation and all that. I was hoping you'd know of a way for me to become a full fury without having to kill someone for it."

"Ah," he said.

I waited for more, but he remained silent.

"Ah? That's it?"

He grinned again.

"You're unique for a fury, Megan. Most of your kind embrace their natural impulses to seek out and punish the wicked."

"So I've been told." I sighed, and it turned into a yawn.

"Do you know why a fury must confront the oldest generation when she comes into her power?" he asked.

"No. And that's a good part of what's pissing me off

about all of this. We do so much without ever understanding why? We're just good little trained sheep, going about our business."

He chuckled.

"I will never be able to see a fury without picturing a sheep, now. Furies kill each other because of their wickedness. The older the fury, the more wickedness she'll have. It's from punishing all the wicked in her lifetime."

"Whoa—whoa—whoa." I lifted my head from the seat. "Are you saying I'm going to get condemned to hell for doing what I was made to do?"

"Yes. But not like every other wicked being you send there. Furies are forgiven their wickedness the moment their wings are ripped from their back, stripping them of their power. They die mortal and have a special resting place in hell. A peaceful one to make up for their restless and angry lives on Earth."

We get peace. But only when we die?

"What the hell? None of this is in the *Book of Fury*."

"There's a Fury book?" he asked, glancing at me. "I'd love to read it."

I studied him for a moment. Given the secrecy in which all creatures guarded information about themselves, and the protection spells on the super-secret library back at the Academy, I knew I should say no. But, I'd also read the book cover to cover and knew it didn't contain much.

"I'll let you read it if you promise to add to it, too."

He waved his hand at me. "What I told you is just common knowledge."

"Not so common if I don't know it. What else do you

know?" I asked, resting my head against the seat again. Sleep was tugging at me, but I didn't want to give in.

"Probably not as much as you'd like. I don't have an answer for your problem. My understanding is that you'll be overcome with rage when you face your great-grandmother. You'll rip her wings away, stripping her of her power, and condemn her to hell. And, in doing so, you'll claim your power."

"Because there can only be three furies," I said with frustration.

"Exactly. Now, tell me something I don't know."

"Furies can only have girls."

"Common knowledge," he said with a smirk.

"Oh yeah? Griffins can only have males."

"Also common knowledge."

I waited for him to connect the dots and knew he had when his smirk faded. He looked thoughtful for a moment.

"Hooking up with Oanen might cause you some trouble."

"Yeah, my mom already tried to talk me out of it. Save your breath."

"I'm not trying to talk you out of anything."

"Then what are you saying?"

"Nothing really," he said with a shrug. "Things that might upset the balance always interest me."

"What balance?" I asked.

"The balance the gods created."

"They're dead."

"Are they?"

"I like talking to you, Zayn. You're smart, and you're not an information hog. Don't start holding back now."

He grinned again, his face illuminating from the headlights of a passing car.

"I'm not holding back," he said. "I really don't know if the gods are dead or not. But if they aren't dead, where are they? Why are they suddenly taking a hands-off approach to the creatures they warred for?"

"Good question. I've been wondering that myself."

"Not many of us have an opportunity to see the inside of a god's realm. When you deliver your first soul, try looking around."

"And report back to you?"

"Nah. It'd be better if you didn't come looking for me after this. But maybe, sometime in the future, I'll stop by and say hi."

I snorted as that potential scene came to life in my head.

"Oh, you showing up on our front stoop will make Oanen so happy," I said.

"Am I detecting some sarcasm?"

"Well, you did leave me naked on a cement floor."

"With a blanket and my jacket. And I didn't look. Well, I did, but in a clinical way to make sure you were okay."

"Yeah, you might not want to ever mention that in front of Oanen." I paused for a moment, thinking of him. "I hope he's okay."

Zayn tapped the wheel with his thumb, deep in thought.

"Griffins are singularly focused on the wellbeing of their mates," he said.

"Don't I know it. And, also, common knowledge."

Zayn looked at me. There wasn't a hint of humor in his eyes.

"You don't understand. Oanen can't be near you when you're fighting her."

Realization hit me hard. Oanen would try to protect me. Not from grandma, but from doing something I would hate myself for. And in doing so, he'd be hurt. Or worse. I'd already seen what fury fire could do to him.

So whatever happened, when I got to grandma's house, I needed to make sure Oanen was gone first. That wasn't going to be easy.

"Thanks," I said softly. "You've helped me more than the people who were supposed to be my guardians and councilors."

"I'm glad. This world can be scary without the right information, skills, or friends." He reached over and set a hand on my shoulder. "If you'll allow me, I'd like to help you sleep. I'll keep you under until we reach her house. You'll wake more rested and ready to face her this way. But the choice is yours."

"Maybe in a little bit. There's something else I wanted to ask you."

He removed his hand.

"Ask away."

"How are you not wicked? There are very few people I've met who've been as clean as you. And they're clean because they're stuck in Uttira and don't do anything. But you're out here, doing things to earn enough money to buy a car like this for your sister."

He chuckled again.

"Thank you for noticing. And for confirming something I have suspected for a long while."

"What's that?"

"In all of our recorded history, and all of the myths and fables, there are many commonalities. Not just in those old faiths and beliefs but in the current ones. And one we have seen over and over again is the concept of redemption.

"I've done wicked things, Megan. But I've always sought to atone for them in some way."

"So you're not wicked because you what? Repented?" I asked, not sure I believed removing wickedness could be that easy.

"No. It's not about being sorry for what I've done. At least, not only that. I do a lot of magic. Not all of it is good. But, I keep track. A mental set of scales, if you will. When the bad starts getting close to the good, I do more good to tip the balance back in my favor."

I considered his words as I stared out the window and watched the stars.

"It all feels like we are set up to play this game. To entertain the gods, you know?"

"I know. Only they stopped watching a long time ago. And I think it's giving us a little bit more room to interpret the rules in our favor."

"And if they start paying attention again?" I asked, looking at him.

His expression didn't change when he answered.

"Then we're all screwed."

He gave me a side glance.

"Except for maybe you, daughter of Hades," he said with a slight smirk.

I smiled in return. Zayn was different. Like he said, neither good nor bad. Just Zayn.

"I think I'm ready for a dose of that Zaynatonin, now."

He reached out and set his hand on my shoulder.

"The things we do to protect those we love shouldn't tip the balance one way or another," he said. "But sometimes, they do. Please remember that when you deal with any wicked in the future."

Before I could ask what he meant, he said, "sleep."

And, I did.

A CRAMP in my neck woke me. With a small cry of pain, I grabbed the mutinying muscle and rubbed lightly as I opened my eyes. The car sat unmoving on the shoulder of some country road, and the driver's seat was empty.

Frowning, I sat up straighter and looked around. It was still dark out and not easy to see far in the moonlight. However, I couldn't see Zayn anywhere. I opened the door and got out to stretch.

"Zayn?" I called.

Nothing but a cool wind answered me.

I bent down and reached into the car for my phone, which was still on the center console so I could check the time.

The screen was open to a draft of a text message.

*Sorry I had to leave. Things are complicated with Elizabeth, and my first priority is keeping her safe. I didn't abandon you, though. Hopefully, the steps I've taken to protect Oanen will keep him safe when you get there. Good luck. Zayn.*

I was so pissed I almost threw my phone. Instead of getting me to Grandma's like he'd promised, he'd ditched me who knew where on the side of the road.

"Eliana was right. Never trust a druid."

It took me a moment to calm down and read the message again. Anger turned to worry. What steps had Zayn taken to protect Oanen?

Pulling up the map app on my GPS, I saw I still had another two hours to drive before I reached Grandma Irene's address. However, the route it wanted me to take sent me directly through the city. I knew better than to try that. I'd have to go around, which meant even more time before I could get to Oanen.

This time, I did throw my phone. Only, I made sure it landed on the front passenger seat. I slammed the door shut, and I stomped around the car to get in behind the wheel. When I started the engine, I saw Zayn had at least left me with a full tank of gas.

Spinning gravel, I took off from the shoulder and listened to the map app's directions.

It wasn't long before I realized I had another problem. I either needed to pull over again and use the ditch or find a gas station. A hungry rumble from my stomach made the decision even though I hated having another delay. According to my map, there was a gas station not far from where I was.

I followed the directions and pulled into a fairly quiet parking lot at the edge of a small town. Wisps of annoyance skimmed over my skin before worming their way underneath it. I wouldn't be able to stay long because douchey people all over the place couldn't just be good.

Growling in agitation, I opened my door and slammed it hard behind me. I cringed, remembering my promise to return the car whole.

"You've got this, Megan. Just breathe."

The door opened, and two teens stepped out. My skin heated, and my temper rose as I walked toward them. The first one had keys in her hand and glanced at me nervously. The second one was engrossed in her phone and barely paying any attention.

"What did you steal?" I demanded, stopping in front of them.

The one with the keys lifted her hands and looked ready to cry.

"I just paid for my gas. I didn't steal anything. I swear."

"Not you. You," I said, staring at the girl with the phone.

The girl with the keys turned on her.

"Did you seriously steal something, Heather?"

The girl looked up in surprise.

"What? No. I was reading the whole time."

"She was," her friend said. "That's all she really ever does."

I studied Heather for a moment. The wickedness didn't lie. She'd done something to break a human or non-human law often enough that I had an urge to hurt her.

"Did you pay for the book you're reading?" I asked.

"Um. No. I downloaded it for free."

"How?"

"I searched for places that had it for free. Usually forums where people share book files."

I rubbed a hand over my face and tried to keep my cool.

"When you're downloading books for free from sites that are posting non-authorized copies that are normally purchased elsewhere for a fee, that's called book piracy and it's stealing. How many books did you download?" The echo of my fury voice had crept into my words.

"One thousand two hundred and twenty-three." She blinked in confusion. "How did I know that?"

"And how much would a book cost if you bothered to buy it."

"Three or four dollars," she said.

"Can you do the math?"

She paled and nodded.

"You've stolen around four thousand dollars and you're what? Only sixteen? I can't wait to see you in another ten years," I said, thinking of Zayn's scales. "You'll be wicked enough by then that I'll be able to do something about it."

I moved to step around them.

"I don't have a lot of money," she said like that made her actions acceptable.

"I don't have a lot of money, either. Does that mean I can walk in this store and just take what I want if the cashier's back is turned? No. You want free entertainment? Turn on the TV and watch the damn news. Stop stealing books."

I went inside without a backward glance and asked for the bathroom key. The attendant gave me a once-over before handing me a chunk of wood with a key attached.

"We have problems with people stealing the key," he said when I gave it a long look.

"Yeah. Seems to be a thing."

When I stepped outside again, the two girls were gone, and I was able to let myself into the restroom without incident. However, I would have been better off on the side of the road.

Shaking my head at the complete sanitary disregard of

the previous toilet users, I wiped off the seat, lined it with toilet paper, and quickly did my business. I tried to touch as little as possible and washed twice before using my elbow to open the door on the way out. It wasn't easy.

When I went back inside, I tossed the key to the cashier.

"Someone needs to go out there and clean that place. It's disgusting."

"If you don't like it, don't use it."

My fingers twitched.

"Don't test me, Anthony," I said. "I'm not in the mood, and I know you've done something wicked, too."

He gave me a startled look.

"How do you know my name?"

I pointed at the name tag on his chest.

Walking away from him, I went to the refrigerator section, hoping for some kind of edible food. There wasn't anything there, but they did have some hot rollers with a taco roll looking thing spinning dryly. Suddenly, I was missing Uttira's healthy food options.

Shaking my head, I took one of the rolls and was about to step away when I was hit from behind with a blast of wicked. I swore under my breath.

Turning slowly, I watched a woman walk in. She was dressed nicely in slacks and a business-type top. Her lipstick and makeup were perfect as was her hair. Yet, the outside didn't matter. Not when I knew the inside was so rotten.

"Don't do it, Megan. Don't do it. Just walk out. You don't have time for this."

I took one step toward the cashier and hesitated as the woman asked for the bathroom key.

The answer to protecting Oanen was right in front of me. If I tried to send this woman to hell, I'd get another burn. I would also have my abilities muted and be unable to sense my grandma's wickedness.

On the flip side, I'd almost killed myself the last time. I thought of the picture of Oanen tied to a tree. Once again, I'd been left with a non- choice.

The woman walked out the door, and I quickly paid for my crappy breakfast and followed.

No one was in the parking lot to see me waiting outside the bathroom door. Or how I grabbed the blond business woman by the throat as soon as the door opened again.

Lifting her high, I embraced my anger.

"Mabel Cartwater, confess." The harsh echo of my words brought forth the woman's sobbing confession.

I listened to how she had repeatedly abused her toddler. Broken wrist. Broken collarbone. Broken femur. All separate occasions. All explained away with childish antics. The worst part was that this sad excuse for a mother was already trying to figure out how to get rid of the kid for good.

Her own child. What was it with shitty moms?

"If this doesn't work," I said, "know that I'll be coming for you."

I let go of my fury power at the same time I squeezed hard.

# CHAPTER SIXTEEN

When I woke up, I was alone on the blacktop outside the restroom. There was no sign of the woman or her car. I swore softly. It didn't matter. I knew her name, and I knew, somehow, I would be seeing her again very soon. The wicked couldn't escape my fury.

Slowly, I got to my feet and winced at the new ache on the side of my neck. Using the key that was lying beside me, I let myself into the bathroom and saw a new burn. The ugly red patch would be impossible to hide.

Leaving the key in the door, I returned to my car. Driving wasn't easy. I had to pull over twice to throw up, and my head felt like it was going to burst. Eventually, I made it around St. Louis to the quiet country subdivisions on the outskirts.

Grandma's house was small compared to its neighbors, but it was well kept. Quaint. I pulled into the driveway and turned off the car.

A flutter of white on the front door caught my attention.

Getting out, I tried to feel for any wickedness. Nothing. Relieved, I went to the door and discovered that the flutter of white was a note for me.

MEGAN,

*Let yourself in. There are cookies on the counter. Make sure you have one and some milk before you come to the backyard.*
*Grandma Irene*

I RIPPED the note from the door.

"What the hell?"

This did not seem like a note from a fury grandma who wanted to kick my ass. The thought made me pause. Never once had I considered if she actually did want to fight me. The book only said that I had to fight her. Maybe she knew I was coming because it was an inevitable thing, not because it was something she wanted. The thought made me frown as I reached for the knob and let myself in.

The scent of freshly baked cookies filled the air. Exactly the smell I would have associated with a normal grandma's house.

Before I made it more than two steps in the direction of the kitchen, I heard the faint sound of pounding. I stopped, tilted my head, and listened.

The sounds seemed to be coming from the hall to my left. I moved that direction, peeking in a bedroom, a bathroom, and then another bedroom. Every room was empty and nicely decorated. Warm and welcoming.

The last door on the left was closed. And from behind it, the banging continued. I hesitated with my hand on the knob. What if sweet, cookie-baking Grandma Irene wasn't in the backyard like the note said? What if this was a trap?

I took a step or two back from the door.

"Hello?" I called, mustering every ounce of fake innocence I possessed.

The banging stopped.

"Megan?" came a familiar, muffled voice from the other side.

"Oanen!" I rushed for the door and flung it open. Before I made it more than a step inside, Oanen had me in his arms. His wind-and-sky scent filled my nose as I inhaled deeply and held on tightly.

"I was so scared," I said. "Are you okay?"

I tried to pull back enough to see for myself, but he wouldn't let me go.

"I'm fine," he mumbled in the crook of my neck. Thankfully, the good side. I shivered at the feel of his breath on my skin.

"I'm so sorry, Megan."

"No. This isn't your fault."

He loosened his hold, and I turned my head to meet his blue gaze. I winced, taking in everything that had changed since I last saw him. The picture on his phone had been right. He had been burned, a look I was familiar with. His eyebrows were a little melted and scorched off. And the faint stink of burnt hair clung to him.

Despite my recent burn, I could feel my fury lift her head.

"What happened? How did my mom find you?" I asked.

"I was at Zayn's house, waiting for the druid to show, when I got a text from an unknown number. I'd given my number out to so many people when we were looking for Zayn that I didn't even think anything of it. The text said to go to the Gizzard. That Zayn was there."

"But he wasn't," I said, already knowing what he would say next.

"No. I can't believe I was so stupid. I walked right into it. Your mom was there, waiting for me. As soon as she touched me, there was a bright flash of light, and I was here in the backyard."

"She teleported?" Even after seeing her disappear in front of me, I had a hard time believing she could teleport. That someday, I would be able to do the same.

"Yeah. She told me to consider myself lucky. That most people who hitched a fury ride went straight to hell."

"And teleporting burned you?"

"No. This was an accident. Your mom had barely finished tying me to the tree out back when the door to the house burst open. Your grandma came marching out, and man was she pissed. She started yelling your mom's name and demanding confessions. Your mom started doing the same. These burns are from the two of them being that close to each other. They were both engulfed in flames. It was like that time next to the car. The only thing that saved me was the tree. Your mom had tied me to the side."

I studied his face and lightly touched the redder spots I had guessed were finger marks.

"And these?" I asked.

"Once your mom disappeared, your grandma came over and demanded to know who I was. I don't think she realized how hot she still was."

I smirked.

"So, you thought my great-grandma was hot?"

He groaned and set his forehead against mine.

"I missed you," he said softly.

"I missed you, too." I tipped my head to lightly kiss his lips. "But I need you to leave."

He made an angry sound and let go of me to gesture at the wall. There were dents the size of a chair in the wall around the door, the windows, even the ceiling. Given the chair that was on the bed, it made sense. No. Not really.

"Um, what were you doing?"

"Trying to break out of here." He ran his hand through his hair and looked at me. "That druid is nothing but trouble, and I still wish you would have been able to send him to hell."

"Explain."

"That insane druid showed up here a few hours ago. I was still tied to the tree in the backyard. Grandma Irene was weeding her garden in the moonlight. She was keeping me company until you arrived."

"Stay on topic, Oanen. What about Zayn?"

"He walked right through her house and out the backdoor like he owned the place. If you think your eyes glow, you should see your grandma's. She had him by the throat before he could blink. And, he calmly informed her that he wasn't trespassing; he was sent to protect Megan's mate."

Oanen reached out and threaded his fingers through mine.

"When your grandma asked who I was, I said I was a close friend. After your mom's reaction about us being together, I wasn't sure telling your grandma more would be wise."

"Yet, you lied to her? What were you thinking?"

"It wasn't a lie. I think I'm one of your closest friends. Aren't I?"

I melted a little and smiled up at him.

"After that shower together, I can't say no."

He frowned slightly.

"I really hope that doesn't mean you plan to shower with all your close friends."

I shrugged indifferently and watched the gold flecks creep into his eyes.

"Are you purposely provoking me?"

"Yes." I smiled sweetly, and he sighed.

"Once your grandma heard that I was your unconsummated mate, things changed. Zayn negotiated a contract with her. I'm locked in this room, unable to leave because of the druid's spell, until you claim your power."

"I don't understand. Why would my grandma agree to that?"

"That's what you don't understand? One, I don't understand what the hell Zayn was doing here. Two, I don't understand why, with all his power, he would lock me in this room instead of just taking me somewhere else. Because I know damn well he can teleport."

"He came to protect you because I asked for his help. The spell will ensure that you stay out of my fight with my grandma. And, I'm pretty sure he couldn't take you without tipping the scales to his wickedness."

I removed my hand from Oanen's and gently kissed his lips. When I pulled back, his golden eyes watched me closely. I saw the moment he caught sight of the new burn.

"Megan, what did you do?"

He reached for me, and I quickly stepped back into the hall.

"Wish me luck," I whispered.

"Megan!" He ran for the opening, hit nothing, and went flying backward. The door slammed shut on its own before he landed.

With a heavy heart, I went to the kitchen, grabbed a cookie, and looked out the window above the sink. The fenced-in yard was large, an acre at least. To the right, near the back, was a single old tree, it's craggy branches barren. To the left was the remnants of this year's garden. The brown, withered plants partially hid the woman bent over in their midst.

I couldn't see exactly what she was doing, but it looked like she was pulling out plants. She held a long handle for something. A support, given her age? Or perhaps a weapon for when I showed up?

The space from the house to the tree was charred. The dry winter grass hadn't stood a chance against whatever happened between my mom and Grandma Irene. I wondered if the same would happen when I stepped outside the door.

I bit into the cookie, wishing I didn't have to test my theories about grandma wanting to fight, wishing there'd been another answer.

"Worthless *Book of Fury*," I murmured, moving toward the back door.

Grandma Irene looked up at the sound of the hinge creaking. An orange light immediately flared to life in her eyes. I felt no fear. No annoyance or anger, either.

"Megan?" she called.

"Yeah. It's me." I walked toward the tree, slow and calm, as she straightened. She wore a long, knit sweater. Something that looked worn and comfortable—over a pair of tan slacks.

"It's a bit late in the year for weeding, isn't it?" I asked. "I mean, I've never gardened, but I would have thought the weeding happened when things were growing."

The orange light flickered in her eyes and went out. Without a word, she set her hoe aside and made her way through the brittle rows to leave her patch of earth. She didn't come closer to me, though. She waited on the normal brown grass, just on the edge of the burnt patch.

I kept walking until about fifteen feet separated us. Close enough to see the true brown color of her eyes and the thick white twist of hair peeking from the back of her head.

With the tree to my right and the house to my left, I faced her and waited for what would happen next.

Her gaze swept me head to toe, lingering on the exposed burn on my neck.

"How many burns do you have, sweetie?" she asked, sounding incredibly kind and loving. It wasn't something I was used to hearing from a motherly figure anymore.

"Five," I said.

"Is the one on your neck the freshest?"

"Yeah. I did it just before coming here. Maybe two hours ago."

Pity filled her gaze.

"On purpose?" she asked.

"Of course."

"Oh, honey," she said sadly. "You're going to burn yourself out trying to fight what you are."

"So I've been told. Repeatedly." I looked around the yard and then at the cookie I still held in my hand. "This is really good, by the way."

"It's a neighbor's recipe that I got a long time ago. Around the great depression."

I looked at the cookie again.

"Wow. That's pretty old."

"Watch it." There was no real anger in her warning. "I was older than you then."

My eyes widened in surprise.

"You've aged really well."

"You have no idea. But you will. You know your boy can't leave that room until you do what needs doing, right?"

"Yeah. I know. That complicates things."

"How so?"

"I don't want to kill you. I don't want to kill anyone just so I can live."

"You're old enough to know that just because you want something, doesn't mean you can have it." She said it sternly but not unkindly. "Like that boy inside."

A flicker of anger burst to life in my belly.

"Don't," I said.

Her eyes sparked orange in response to my warning tone. She didn't look angry, though.

"I knew it wouldn't last long," she said. "Not when you're this close to me. I have dealt out punishments and delivered the wicked to hell for too long for you not to sense it. It's who we are. What we're made for. And that's why you need to let the boy go when we're done here. He's not right for you."

"You don't know that."

"I do. Our kind can only have girls. His kind can only have boys. Furies and griffins aren't meant to mix. And trust me when I say you want the next generation to be born. You won't want to punish the wicked forever."

Every word she spoke against my relationship with Oanen burrowed further under my skin and fueled the ball of anger growing in my middle.

"There has to be another way," I said stubbornly.

"Of course there is. Sleep with a human. They're very fertile and easy to leave."

The idea of being with someone other than Oanen ripped at my insides. We had already begun our bond. We were committed on a level I didn't fully understand. Even now, I could feel his worry and fear for me. And his love. What she was suggesting would be cheating.

I fisted my hands against her irreverent proposal and struggled to maintain control over my actions and thoughts.

"I meant there has to be another way to gain my power. A way that doesn't involve killing you. It isn't fair to punish you for something you couldn't stop yourself from doing.

The gods made you this way. And, I'll hate myself for continuing their unjust system."

"I understand. I've hated myself for over one hundred years, now. I wish you could be spared that. But you can't. Now, if you want your winged friend freed, you better stop trying to deny what you're feeling and do what you're meant to do."

"No," I said through clenched teeth.

"Oh? You don't care about him? Well, that's a good thing because he hasn't had anything to eat or drink since he's gotten here."

The rage grew.

"I know you're baiting me," I said, trying to deny the anger.

"No, this is baiting you." She smiled, a curl of her lips that held no humor. "I knew I would burn your boy when I touched him."

I couldn't stop the fury consuming me, and once the wrong done to Oanen brought it to life, I could feel every bit of wickedness coming from the old woman standing across from me. The need to punish her consumed me.

"Irene Firestorm, hell awaits you," I said, my double-edged voice rattling the branches of the scorched tree.

"Come take your birthright, fledgling. If you think you're able." She lifted her arms slightly. Flames ignited at her fingertips and slowly spread up her arms and over her shoulders to catch at her back.

Like when I'd faced my mother, I could feel the heat as wings burst forth from her back. These weren't the tiny wings I'd seen in the picture of myself at the lake but huge, beautiful wings that danced with the flames of hell.

The grass at the old fury's feet started to smoke. To me, the white wisps acted like cannon fire for our fight to start.

The rage inside me demanded that I scream my anger and launch myself at her. I shook with the need to hurt her. To rip her wings from her back. To make her bleed in retribution for her actions.

In my mind, I could see the countless wicked she'd punished and delivered to hell. The image of her face was burned further into my mind with each trip to the underworld.

My steps slowed.

There was no joy in her expression. Resolution. Anger. Impatience. So many other emotions. But never any joy.

"Don't fight it, Megan. It will kill you."

I focused on my grandmother's blazing eyes and saw the same thing now. So many emotions. Most of all, pity.

I couldn't stop my forward movement. I couldn't hold back the rage as I reached her or the tears that began a slow trek down my face.

"My poor fledgling," Irene said, opening her arms wider.

I walked right into them and let her wrap me in a hug even as I reached for her wings.

"Do what you must," she whispered in my ear.

Gripping the base of her right wing I pulled hard. She gasped, but didn't try to hurt me in return. Instead, she comforted me, running a hand over the back of my head.

"Good girl," she said, her words raspy with pain.

The wing shrunk in my hand, the power piercing my palm and filling me with its heady weight. I didn't just hunger for more. My fury needed it. I could feel how broken I was now. All the burns on my skin weren't just burns but holes in my existence. The power was working to fill them. To fix me. Without the other wing, I would die.

Knowing that, even with my need to hurt her still consuming me, I fought against myself as I reached for the other wing. I shook in her arms.

"Shh, now. It's almost over," she said.

"It will never be over," I said as I gripped her remaining wings. "I will never forgive the gods for forcing this on me."

I pulled hard, stripping her of her remaining power.

She slumped against me, and suddenly I was the one supporting her. I barely noticed her weight.

Hate and power consumed me. A new fire seared through my veins, ripping me apart and rebuilding me into something infinitely stronger than what I had been. Twin infernos sprouted from my back and grew into wings large enough to wrap around us.

In the cocoon of their flames, I could feel a pull, something urging me to allow the earth to swallow me whole. But, I ignored it, unwilling to let it distract me from the thought filling my mind. Eras. The incubus from the Roost, who had been harassing Zoe and Kelsey. He'd been wicked but his crimes petty, not wicked enough to send him to hell.

I remembered my words to him. *Make amends and cleanse your slate.*

I'd gone the other way with the girl at the gas station. I'd told her I couldn't wait for a few more years for her theft.

The druid had been right. Our deeds were being

weighed on a scale that only a few could sense. Tip the scale, and go to hell. But, who decided what deeds went on each side of the scale? I realized it wasn't who but what. Our laws and rules determined the wicked.

And just like that, the view of my world shifted.

# CHAPTER SEVENTEEN

I RELEASED MY HOLD ON MY GRANDMOTHER AND LET HER slump to the ground. She looked up at me with her dull brown eyes. Sweat beaded her forehead, and her pale skin was starting to redden. Yet, I saw no fear in her gaze.

"Irene Firestorm, you are condemned to a mortal life and are assured your peaceful resting place in hell."

She struggled to her feet, and I yearned to comfort her like she'd comforted me. Instead, I took several healthy steps back from her.

"But it is not your time," I said, my rage vanishing.

The back door banged open and Oanen came running out.

I held up my hand.

"Wait. Give me a minute to cool off," I said.

He stopped, his gaze shifting to my grandma who was looking at me with shock.

"What have you done?" she asked.

"Exactly what I was supposed to do."

"No, you were supposed to deliver me to hell to seal your power."

"I do not need to be told the laws set forth by humans and non-humans, alike, because I know them the moment they are created or changed. They are in me. They are who I am as much as I am hell's judge, jury, and executioner. And, I can interpret them as I choose.

"To obtain my power, I must strip it from the first living generation. To seal my newly acquired power, a wicked soul must be delivered to hell. There is nothing written that says that soul must be yours or that you must die when I strip you of power."

Knowing I was cooler, I went to the woman who'd welcomed me with cookies then provoked me to spare me.

"As a human, you've done nothing wicked. Your slate is wiped clean. Your remaining days are your own."

"But, the soul, Megan."

I smiled, my mind already seeking the soul I needed.

"Will you keep an eye on Oanen for me? He tends to go missing when I'm not at his side."

She nodded once, and I let the image of the woman from the gas station fill my mind. Her perfect hair, her pristine makeup, her nice clothes, and her foul, foul soul. As my wings sprouted and wrapped around me, I saw her clearly. Not because of a memory, but because I could see what she was doing at that exact moment. She was driving her car on a road in the city. I could feel her thoughts and knew what she was planning. She'd waited for her husband to drop their son off at daycare, and now she was on her way to pick him up again. The boy would die.

I listened to the pull of the earth and let myself sink into the darkness. I had form, but nothing else around me did. One moment, it felt like I was falling in a void; the next, I was rising. All the while, the woman, where she was and what she was doing, never left my mind. I could feel myself drawing closer to her. A moment before the darkness disappeared, instinct had me squatting down into a sitting position.

My sudden appearance in her passenger seat startled a shriek from her. She jerked the wheel and sent the car careening into a tree. It was a big tree, and she'd been in a hurry to end her son's life.

I listened to every snap of bone as the metal crunched. I flew forward too, the airbags cushioning any blow, not that I needed it. I was officially a favored daughter of hell, now. Very little could touch me.

When the car settled, I looked at the woman. Her head slowly turned toward me. Vessels had burst in her eyes.

"I take no joy in condemning you," I said. "But by doing so, I have saved a life and maintained my balance."

A rattling breath escaped her as I reached forward. Like the void I had used to get to her, she seemed to lose substance. I could see a soft blue-white glow radiating inside of her. It extended in an oval from her head to her heart, the center of it at the base of her throat. I grabbed the glow in my fist and let my wings close around us.

The same sensation of being pulled downward filled me but more strongly this time. I fell into the void, the soul still in my grasp. The woman looked at me with a mix of terror and anger in her eyes. If not for the way my fingers lingered within the illusion of her neck, I would have thought she was alive.

The heat of my wings stayed wrapped around me as we plunged downward. Outside their flaming protection, the temperature dropped until we slowed.

Below me, the darkness began to fade to reveal a vast expanse of black ice, underlit by the faint flicker of blue flame. The soul jerked in my grasp, a wisp of nothing that had no real strength.

Her gaze drifted from mine to look at the world around us, and I did the same. To the left, a land covered in snow and mountains and storms. To the right, a golden flame lit the top of a towered fortress at the bottom of another tall mountain.

As soon as I saw the flame, I knew that was where I was meant to go.

I opened my wings and soared in that direction. My wings didn't flap to propel me forward; thought moved me. With incredible speed, I crossed the black ice and reached a black, rocky shore, seemingly devoid of life.

Far below, rivers of glowing orange and red twined through the rock in a meandering path toward the fortress. At first, I thought the streams were molten lava. Then, I heard the faint screaming and looked closer. Souls, twisted and tortured, writhed in channels of fire and blood. Like the soul I now carried, they all had form.

The sight of them didn't bother me. I knew every soul in those hell rivers had earned its place. But that wasn't where this soul belonged. There was a place for every level of wicked. The streams were for the worst. And this one wasn't the worst.

A rumble came from the side of the fortress. Something white moved against the black. And, as I neared, I could have sworn it was a man in a robe, pushing a boulder uphill. However, I was too far away to be sure.

The soul and I flew over the streams to the fortress, itself. The dark spires were silent and unwelcoming. None stood out more so than the others, yet I knew just where to go. After reaching my destination, I entered through a window, tucking in my wings to land lightly on my feet. The barren entry point, lit by torches, was as cold and dank as the hall leading from it.

With the soul at my side, thanks to my steady grip, I led her to a door. Everything I'd done so far had been instinctual. A knowing of rightness. And, now, I knew I was almost done. Instead of opening the door, I pushed the soul toward it. She struggled, her hands traveling through my arms even though I could grip her by the base of her throat. She passed through the wooden barrier as if it didn't exist. I released my hold and withdrew my empty hand.

Soul delivered. A ripple of ease shook my still visible wings, and I felt complete. Whole and healthy.

A scrape of noise down the hall drew my attention. In the flicker of torchlight, a pale specter leaned against the stone and stared at me. She looked like Ashlyn's doppelganger right out of the Grecian era, based on her flowing white dress. She lifted a hand and pointed at me, her lips moving. Like the soul I just delivered, no sound came out of her mouth.

I felt the tug again, pulling me upward, telling me not to linger. Turning on my heel, I retraced my steps down the hall and jumped out of the window. My wings expanded, and I soared upward into the void once more.

Oanen filled my thoughts, and I found myself in

Grandma's backyard once more. My wings disappeared, and I looked around at the destruction of her yard. Most of the plants on the outside of her garden had burned away to ash.

The back door creaked.

"Don't you worry about any of that, Megan. Come inside and have another cookie."

I glanced at my great-grandmother, a woman I didn't really know. Yet, she'd given me so much in a brief period of time. And, it wasn't only her power that she'd given. She'd given me more understanding and comfort than anyone else I could remember, outside of Oanen and Eliana.

"Thank you," I said, moving toward her. "I hope you'll still be able to garden next year."

"I will. That ash will make the soil richer." She paused until I was closer to the door.

"What did you think of it?"

"Hell?"

"Yes."

"I guess it's just what I thought it should be. Cold, dark, depressing."

"Only the part furies visit," she replied.

"There's more?"

She smiled. "There's a lot you still don't know. And, now, there's someone who can tell you about it. If you'd like."

"I would. You have no idea how much."

"I might," she said with a small smile. "Would you like to stay for lunch?"

She opened the door and motioned me inside. The sight

of Oanen pacing the kitchen while speaking on the phone prevented me from answering her.

"The answer hasn't changed. Megan said she didn't sense his wickedness, and I trust her." Seeing me, he paused his pacing. I walked up to him, kissed him lightly on the lips and stole the phone.

I put it on speaker just in time to hear Adira's reply.

"While he may not be wicked yet, he could become wicked. The kind of magic that requires souls can be dangerous, Oanen. He needs to be found and brought in for questioning."

"That's your decision," I said. "However, Oanen and I will not be the ones tracking him down."

"Respectfully, Fury, Oanen accepted a position as enforcer for the Council."

Irene waved her hands to gain my attention and mouthed, "use the voice."

"Accepting such a role," Adira said, "means he must heed the direction given by the Council to—"

"Enough," I said sharply. It wasn't the double fury voice, just the annoyed Megan voice. I shrugged at Irene at the same time Adira started speaking again.

"We acknowledge that you were unable to sense his wickedness, but that doesn't absolve us of our obligation to determine what he is planning to do with all that life energy."

Irene reached over and tapped the base of my throat.

"There," she said softly.

"From now until the end of time, Oanen belongs to me," I said, my voice ringing with the full power of a fury. "Any task he chooses to perform on behalf of the Council, he does with me at his side. And since I have spent time with Zayn Sias and have found him to be completely without any trace of wickedness, I will not waste my time tracking him down. Casting spells with life energy is not against the laws of Mantirum or mankind. Your persistence in finding the druid seems unusually driven. I think, perhaps, I would like to question you about that as well as your insistence in naming Nicolette Barchim guilty of a crime she was proven not to have committed."

Grandma Irene laughed silently beside Oanen, who watched me with his steady golden gaze. However, no indication of what Adira was thinking or feeling came from the other end of the call for several long moments.

"We understand your warning," she said finally. "Congratulations on your ascension, Fury."

"Thanks, Adira," I said in my normal voice. "We'll see you soon."

She started stammering, and with a wide grin on my face, I hung up on her.

"That felt so good," I said. "I think she might be peeing herself right now."

"You know they're going to try to find reasons to keep you out of Uttira," Oanen said.

"And they won't be able to," Grandma Irene said. "We've been using that house to raise our young for a very long time."

"That was a really cool trick, by the way," I said. "The only time I've ever been able to use that voice is when I was angry."

"Stick around, and I'll teach you plenty more cool tricks. Some, your mom might not even know."

"I'd like that very much."

We helped Grandma Irene prepare a simple lunch of sandwiches then spent the next few hours getting to know each other. She was a fount of knowledge as she guided me in the responsibilities of my new role and how I would now be perceived by the rest of the world.

"Speaking of perception, I think it's about time you called your mother," she said.

I made a face.

"I'm not sure I'm ready to talk to her yet. She took Oanen."

"And I burned him," Grandma said with a shrug. "We both did what we needed to do in order to help you become what you are."

This time, hearing it didn't send me into a rage because I really did believe her.

"You, maybe. But, Mom was pretty clear in her opinion of my relationship with Oanen."

Grandma nodded slowly and moved the plate of cookies in my direction.

"So was I," she said.

"And now?"

She glanced at Oanen, winking at him.

"I can see that a simple break isn't possible. And a complex one could be detrimental to a fury who just acquired her powers. What happens next is up to the gods. I only hope, for your sake, there will be future generations because you won't want to deliver souls forever."

I didn't think making occasional trips to hell would be so bad if it meant an eternity with Oanen.

"And what about Mom," I asked. "Is she going to try to take him again?"

"No. She won't risk going anywhere near you now." She paused with a frown. "Well, maybe she won't. You've proven that two furies can be in the same place and not kill each other. However, you may not want to test that theory, again."

It made me a little sad that I might not ever see my mom again. And suddenly, I understood why she'd deserted me.

"She was sensing my powers, wasn't she? Just before she left me in Uttira," I said.

"She held out longer than any mother before her. She loved you very much."

I took the phone from the table, and both Grandma Irene and Oanen excused themselves.

Knowing Mom hadn't just ditched me for no reason made dialing harder. Nerves made my hands sweaty. I remembered every shitty feeling I'd had toward her. Not once had I really thought of all the meals she'd made me before she'd left, the clean laundry that had just magically appeared in my drawers or all the times she had stuck up for me at school when I'd been caught fighting. Granted, it hadn't felt like that at the time, but I could see it now.

The phone rang twice before she picked up.

"Is it done?" she asked.

"I've delivered my first soul to hell and sealed my power."

She exhaled heavily.

"I'm so proud of you, baby."

The words touched me deeply since I now understood how much she meant them.

"Thanks, Mom."

"Now, you need to ditch the boy. I know it'll be hard but—"

"No, Mom. I won't leave him."

"Megan," she said with warning.

"There's something you should know. I didn't kill Grandma Irene."

"What?" Shock quieted her next word. "Impossible."

"Maybe for some. I guess I just saw things a little differently. She's mortal now. But if you can't believe that her deeds as a fury are the faults of the gods, you should probably stay away from her. Just in case."

She hesitated a moment.

"I promise not to make any plans to say hello. She's earned her remaining days of peace. But, finding a way around sending her to hell doesn't change your need to leave the griffin boy."

"Are you sure?" I asked. "Sparing Grandma was supposed to be impossible. Who's to say a relationship with a griffin needs to be thought of the same way? Has anyone actually tried it?"

Mom was quiet.

"If it's a mistake, let me make it," I said. "I just want to know that you'll leave him alone."

She chuckled softly.

"You're a full fury now. I know better than to meddle in person." She paused for a moment. "Will you call me again? Let me know how things are going?"

"I'll call you daily if you want."

"I'd like that very much."

I hung up smiling and turned to find Oanen just behind me.

"I could feel your worry," he said. "And then your joy."

"We need to talk more about how this feelings thing works."

He nodded slowly.

"We'll have plenty of time tonight. Are you ready to go back to the condo?"

"Almost. First, we need to return the car I borrowed."

Saying goodbye to Grandma Irene was bittersweet. She made me promise that I'd pop in whenever I needed advice or information.

"I know you can use the phone," she said. "But I missed out on a lifetime of having family. I want to see you as much as I can, now. And with your wings, you can be here in a blink, so there's no excuse."

And that turned into a quick lesson on how I could travel from place to place through the void, which wasn't actually a void but the entrance of the underworld that connected to everywhere.

I PULLED to a stop in front of Elizabeth Sias' house and killed the engine. The car, as promised, was in the same pristine condition that it had been when I'd borrowed it.

"We're here," I said softly, looking over at Oanen.

We'd opted to take turns driving instead of stopping for a room somewhere. He'd driven most of the way, only letting me take the wheel a few hours before.

When he heard my voice, he sat up and rubbed a hand over his hair.

"I'm going to return the keys, then we can go," I said.

"How are we getting back to the condo from here?" he asked.

"Your choice. You can fly us or I can," I said with a grin before getting out.

It was just after dawn, but I hoped Elizabeth would be up.

The street was quiet as I let myself through the gate and up to the house. A prickle of awareness tickled the back of my neck, and I looked around. It felt like I was being watched, but I didn't see anything. And, either gaining my wings had toned down the volume on my wicked sensor, or there were less of them around.

The curtain moved, distracting me from my thoughts.

I smiled and went up to the door to knock softly. It opened a moment later.

Elizabeth looked over my shoulder.

"You found him," she said.

"I did. And I'm returning your car in one piece as promised."

I held out the keys. She shook her head.

"Toss them to me."

I did.

"I also have a message," I said quickly. "The Council wants to question Zayn. I let them know that Oanen and I wouldn't be involved in that. But, I wouldn't put it past them to send someone else. Zayn should make himself scarce for a while. Will you tell him?"

She nodded.

"Thanks for the car, and tell your brother thanks for his help," I said, turning away.

"And thank you for yours," she said before closing the door.

Oanen waited for me on the sidewalk.

"Ready?" I asked.

## CHAPTER EIGHTEEN

"I'VE BEEN READY FOR A LONG TIME," OANEN SAID, HIS EYES golden. "I think you can get us home faster."

My stomach did a happy twist, and I reached for his hand. Traveling through the void was almost instantaneous now that I knew how to focus.

As soon as we appeared in the condo, I released him. Every nerve ending was tingling, and it had nothing to do with our trip through hell's gate and everything to do with how Oanen was looking at me now.

"I love you, Oanen Quill," I said.

His gaze heated further.

"I don't know about you, but I could use a shower," he said.

Images of the last time we took a shower together flitted through my head.

"Are you sure you're not hungry first?" I asked.

"Oh, I'm hungry," he said.

I knew what he meant, and a moment's nervousness claimed me before I realized how pointless it was. All the time I'd hesitated and held myself back from him had almost cost us a life together.

I gave Oanen a soft smile and removed my jacket. He echoed the move and tossed his on the couch.

"Interested in a movie?" I asked, kicking off my shoes.

"Only if you are," he said, doing the same thing.

My pulse started to pick up speed.

"Maybe. It's hard to decide what I want to do now that we're back and I'm not tired, or hurt, or distracted."

I walked toward him and was thrilled at the sight of his pupils dilating.

"I heard there are some impressive views in New York. Maybe we should go sightseeing," I said.

Setting my hands on his shoulders, I stood on my toes to brush my lips against his. He groaned and started encircling me in his arms. I quickly twisted out of his grasp.

He didn't move to chase me but watched me hungrily as I backed toward the bedroom.

"Although, it is early. And not all the attractions might be ready for viewing. I think you were right the first time," I turned so I could watch where I was walking.

"I'm going to go take a shower," I said over my shoulder. "Know any best friends who might want to join me?"

I squealed when I was picked up and tossed over his shoulder.

"I love teasing-Megan," he said, stroking a hand over my butt.

"Then you're really going to love today."

WRAPPED IN OANEN'S ARMS, I idly trailed my fingers over his pectorals and circled his nipple. Images of what we'd done repeatedly over the past few hours, flitted through my mind and rekindled the fire that burned inside of me only for Oanen.

"If you keep thinking like that, we're never going to leave this place. And, you need to eat."

I grinned and let the images keep playing in my mind until I found myself on my back, pinned under a very eager Oanen.

He kissed me hard then stared down at me.

"Thank you for finally saying yes," he said.

"Thank you for breaking the world's record for fastest trip to the store."

He grinned at me. "I promised no babies, and I meant it. You're all I want, Megan. Now and forever."

His love for me filled my mind.

"And if I want babies later?" I asked, growing more comfortable with the plural form of the hypothetical.

"Then, I'll want them, too."

"And you're okay practicing until then?" I wriggled under him enticingly. He groaned and playfully dropped down on me, his weight enough to smother a human but not me.

"Feed me." His words were muffled by the mattress.

I laughed and poked him in the ribs.

"I know you're only saying that because you heard my stomach growl."

He lifted himself and grinned down at me. A real smile, full and true. Not only did I see his humor, I felt it all the way down to my toes.

"You're right," he said. "And, I can't help it. This need to care for you is…"

"Awful? Stifling? Nauseating?"

"Too new and thrilling," he said. "You're mine, Megan. Finally. And I'm doing everything I can to make sure you never regret that."

He kissed me again then rolled off me and stood beside the bed.

I couldn't help but openly stare.

"Sightseeing?" he asked.

"Yep. New York sure has a lot to boast about."

He held out a hand.

"Let's shower and decide where we want to eat. We can go anywhere now, thanks to my amazing, slightly ornery, but completely adorable mate."

"Honestly, I'm ready to get home," I said. "I want to find out what's going on with Fenris and Eliana." I sat up quickly. "Crap. I forgot to call Eliana."

Ignoring the naked golden god at my side, I grabbed my phone from the nightstand and dialed Eliana.

"Hey, Megan," she answered.

"Hey. Sorry I didn't call sooner. It's been crazy."

Oanen trailed a finger down my arm, a reminder of how that "crazy" had ended.

"I heard," Eliana said with a light laugh. "You ruffled some feathers with your Oanen-is-mine speech."

I grinned. "Good. They need to stop toying with people."

"Agreed."

"Good news, though. Oanen and I are heading back to

Uttira today." I bit my lip as I remembered something. "As soon as we find his car," I asked.

"Um, you might want to rethink that," she said.

"What? Finding his car?"

"No. Coming back to Uttira."

"Don't you love me anymore?" I tried to say it jokingly but couldn't ignore the insecurity I was feeling.

"Like crazy," she said. "And that's why I want you to go somewhere else for a while. Somewhere romantic and amazing where you and Oanen can do all the new couple things you're probably already doing. When you get it out of your system, you can come back."

I was quiet for a moment, feeling a little hurt.

"You're afraid of being around us," I said.

"Yes and no. I'd be fine with one of you at a time. But, wanting you to stay away has more to do with my mom. New couples are too tempting. You give off too much energy."

"You mean sexual energy." I loved finally being with Oanen, but I missed Eliana, too. It felt like I'd unintentionally picked between the two of them.

"Yes," Eliana said. "That. And with Mom being pregnant, I just don't want to worry about you."

I looked at Oanen, who was watching me closely.

"How long do we need to stay away?" I asked.

"Mom's due in five months, but I don't think it'll take that long for your new, um…lust to wear off."

Five months? I had hated being trapped in Uttira. Yet, now that I was free to come and go, Eliana was telling me I shouldn't. I couldn't imagine staying away from her for that long.

Oanen motioned for the phone, and I handed it over.

"Eliana, Megan needs to see you as much as you need to see her. We'll stay away for two weeks. Then we're coming home." His golden eyes pinned me, and he handed back the phone.

I quickly put it to my ear.

"Eliana?" I said.

"Yep, I'm still here. I'm glad the bossy griffin is officially in your hands," she said. "It'll be weird not having a male protectively hovering all the time, but I'm sure I'll manage."

I tried biting my lip again while fighting not to say something. But, my meddling, happily mated self couldn't control herself.

"You never know. There might be someone lurking in the shadows, waiting to take up that mantle."

She snorted.

"I hope not. I'll see you in two weeks," she said. "Hopefully, Mom will have lost interest in what Uttira has to offer by then and go back to New York."

I smiled, already anticipating the Fenris and Eliana details I would get when I saw her next.

"I'll see you in two weeks," I said.

# EPILOGUE

With a critical eye, I considered the house.

"What do you think?" Oanen called from his position on the roof. A pair of shorts hung low around his hips. It didn't matter how much time had passed, he looked tempting as hell.

"I think you need to get down from there and give me a foot rub."

He grinned, tossed the paintbrush he held into the can beside him, and jumped from the roof. Landing with his usual grace, he strode toward me so he could set his hands on my rounded belly.

"The baby being a troublemaker again?"

"No. I just wanted you to hold me."

Oanen kissed me then slipped his arms around me so we stood looking at our newly painted house. I would miss the obnoxious rainbow colors that had decorated it, but it was time to move on and grow up. The soft buttercream color definitely made the house look less crazy and more welcoming.

"Things will be different for this next generation," he said, tightening his hold just a smidge.

"I know." We'd talked at length before taking this next step. "If this baby is a girl, she'll be raised knowing exactly what she is."

The newly rewritten *Book of Fury* would be her bedtime story. And when her anger started, she would live with her Auntie Eliana instead of being left alone. Not a day would go by where she would question my love for her. Well, not more than a week.

"And, if it's a boy," I said, "I'll build a coop."

Oanen chuckled behind me and pressed a kiss to my temple. Despite his outward affection, I could feel the worry that he was trying so hard to hide from me.

"I don't regret this decision," I said, twisting in his arms to look up at him. He had barely aged a day. Neither of us had.

It'd taken me a while to understand my Grandma Irene's words about needing the next generation. Watching all of our friends age, while time stood still for us, had been eye opening. As much as I worried about the gender, I didn't fear having a baby. Not anymore.

"If this one's not a girl, we'll try again," Oanen said.

"And again? And again? And again?" I asked playfully.

"I'm willing to sacrifice my evenings until we get it right." The husky note in his voice made me shiver.

"Except tonight," I said. "Our friends will be here in a few hours. You have paint to clean up, and I have a dinner to make."

"Get to it, woman," he said with a playful swat to my butt. "First one done gets a foot rub."

I bolted for the house. It was probably more of a waddled hustle, but I worked with what I had.

However, instead of going to the kitchen, I went to the study and pulled the new and improved *Book of Fury* from the shelf. It was much thicker than its predecessor and was filled with not only my handwriting, but Grandma Irene's, Grandma Grace's, and my mom's as well.

I thought of Grandma Irene, who had recently passed away. I missed her terribly, but thanks to her, I had a relationship with the other two furies. A long distance one, but I'd take it. And also, thanks to Grandma Irene, I had hope for my own future and that of my future daughter's.

I opened the book and read a passage I'd written for the next generation.

*WHILE IT'S true there can only be three Furies, it's not necessary to kill the elder generation. It is only necessary to strip her of her power by ripping off her wings. It won't be easy to stop there. You'll want to condemn her to hell for her crimes against the wicked. But remember not to hold her at fault. It is the gods who made us the way we are. And while we can control some of our impulses, others cannot be refused.*

*Embrace who you are and take your power when you're ready. Remember that you will not age until you do. You will watch the lives of your friends move with time but you will remain standing still until you bring forth the next generation of fury.*

I CLOSED the book and placed it on the shelf. The gods made

us, gave us our gifts, and left us to make our own choices. And, I'd made mine. I had no regrets.

"Megan?" Oanen called, the back-door slamming. "I think I won."

"Does that mean I don't get a foot rub?" I asked, coming out of the office.

He gave me a wry grin.

"It means I help with dinner, and you get a foot rub afterward."

I smiled at him.

Nope. I didn't have a regret in the world.

THANK you for reading *Fury Freed*, the conclusion to the *Of Fates and Furies* series. Want to know more about what's going on with Eliana and Fenris? You're in luck! I'm already working on the first book in the *By Kiss and Claw* series. Keep reading for a little peek from Fenris' point of view. And, if you want to hear when it's ready, just sign up for my newsletter at https://melissahaag.com/subscribe/. Happy reading!

# BONUS SCENE

**Fenris...**

I walked around Megan's house, inhaling deeply. It'd barely been an hour since she and Oanen had left and a little more than that since Eliana's departure. Not enough time to lose either of their scent trails this far out of town.

I focused on Eliana's sweet scent and followed it from the driveway to the backdoor. A hunger surged forward. A need to touch. To taste. I clenched my fists, tired of just inhaling her. If only she were here.

The urge to howl my frustration rose, stifling common sense. But only for a moment. I exhaled slowly and reminded myself why I couldn't give into any of my urges. Eliana wasn't ready. She needed more time.

When she finally did run from me, I needed it to be because she wanted me to chase her, not because she was afraid.

I pulled my phone from my pocket and sent a text.

*First security sweep done. Megan's car is still here and unmaimed.*

While Megan's abandonment caused me some serious issues—how was I going to get my Eliana fix now?—there was a silver lining. I now had a valid reason to stay in contact with Eliana.

A message appeared as I stared at my phone.

*They just left. Of course her car is still fine.*

An intense satisfaction coursed through me reading her words, and I paced Megan's snow dusted lawn as I responded.

*It doesn't hurt to be cautious. How's your car?*

*My car is fine. Go home, Fenris.*

*I'll see you Monday.*

I waited for a minute, and when nothing came through, I smiled and pocketed my phone. I hadn't really expected her to respond.

Patience and a plan would get me what I desperately wanted. Good thing I had both. It wouldn't be much longer before Eliana was begging me to howl and chase her through the woods.

Whistling a jaunty tune, I stripped from my clothes, bundled them together, and shifted.

It was time to put my plan in motion.

What a ride! I loved embarking on a new world and hope you enjoyed it enough to want more. Megan was so kickass to write and Eliana's stories are gearing up to be quite epic.

Since you're here and still reading, I'm hoping I can take another minute of your valuable time to tell you something that's near and dear to me…it took over 600 hours to write this series! Yep, that's a lot of hours. It's crazy the amount of time an author can spend creating the stories you love. But can you imagine working your job for 600 hours and not getting paid by your employer? It would suck sweaty monkey balls.

While I do occasionally run discounts on my books to entice new readers, please never download my books from sites offering them for free when they are otherwise paid books. It's called book piracy and hurts the literary economy more than you know. Mainly the authors.

If you're strapped for cash, the legal and most beneficial way to support any author you love, is to go to your local library and request they add a book (or a million) to their digital lending library. Libraries usually get discounts, so they rarely say no!

So, in summary, I love you for reading, but I'll love you even more if you're reading a legal copy that fairly reimburses the author for the time spent writing.

And please don't forget, if you loved this series, let me and other readers know by leaving a review on the retailer site of your choice.

Happy reading!

Melissa

*Touch*
*Moved*
*Warwolf*
*Nephilim*

# BOOKS BY M.J. HAAG

## (MELISSA HAAG'S ADULT PEN NAME)

*M.J. Haag books are not meant for readers under 18 or those who are offended by sex-loving tree nymphs, beasts who truly deserved to be cursed, or zombies (whaaaattt? Yeah, I know...).*

### Beastly Tales
*(Beauty and the Beast retelling!)*

*Depravity*

*Deceit*

*Devastation*

### Tales of Cinder
*(Cinderella retelling!)*

Disowned (Prequel)

Defiant

### Resurrection Chronicles
*(zombies and hottie demons!)*

*Demon Ember*

*Demon Flames*

*Demon Ash*

*Demon Escape*

*Demon Deception*

*Demon Night*

**More to come!*